"Where do we start, Charlie?"

Charlie gave a small, unsteady laugh. "Maybe I'll leave that up to you."

"All right." Cole's eyes bored into hers, making her feel vulnerable and somehow very sexy. "I have a feeling you'd appreciate a straightforward approach. Am I wrong?"

Charlie sipped her coffee, stalling for time. "I think that depends on the subject, Cole."

"I want you, Charlie. I want your friendship. I want laughter and talk and trust. I want us to have evenings together, weekends. I want to make love—"

"Cole . . . you're moving too fast."

"Am I? All right, I'll slow down. But I'm sure you get my drift." He eased across the couch and framed Charlie's face in his hands.

"How's Sunday?" he asked in a husky voice. "Your house or mine?"

Carrie Hart, who has also been published as Jackie Merritt, started writing romances four years ago, after working as an accountant most of her life. She's proud of having had the courage to make such a radical career change. Proud, too, of her family's long history in the lumber business, which inspired the passionate story of Charlie and Cole in *Hard-Headed Woman*.

Hard-Headed Woman
CARRIE HART

Harlequin Books

TORONTO • NEW YORK • LONDON
AMSTERDAM • PARIS • SYDNEY • HAMBURG
STOCKHOLM • ATHENS • TOKYO • MILAN

FORTY YEARS OF
Romance

Published May 1989

ISBN 0-373-25352-4

1

THE U.S. FOREST SERVICE'S administration building in Missoula, Montana was an austere structure, appearing utilitarian both inside and out with its bland, emotionless green paint. It was a place Charlotte "Charlie" McAllister had become very familiar with over the past eight years. As a sawmill owner, Charlie attended every federal timber auction, although for the past two years she'd been one of the unsuccessful bidders.

Not only her, though, Charlie acknowledged with a pang as she stepped into the designated auction room and saw only two people waiting for today's proceedings. Only a scant two years ago every timber sale had been attended by six to eight potential buyers. Now, other than Pete Dirksen, one of the two men who had preceded her arrival, every one of the small sawmillers in the area had gone out of business.

The other man in the room was Rick Slaughter, and the hair on the back of Charlie's neck prickled as she regarded Canfield Lumber Company's timber supervisor. All the small sawmill owners in the area blamed Canfield for their troubles, but there was certainly nothing illegal about the huge company winning all the recent timber contracts. The problem had to do with volume and cost efficiency; Canfield was simply in a position to pay more for timber than a small company could.

Charlie felt both men's eyes on her, Pete's lighting up in friendly recognition, Rick's doing a slow study that galled

Charlie no end. Every time she saw Rick Slaughter, he stared as though speculating on the color of her underwear, and it never failed to rile Charlie. She'd never liked that sort of look from any man.

With a nod at Rick, Charlie walked over to Pete. "Morning, Pete." She took a chair beside the elderly man.

Pete Dirksen grinned wryly. "Ready for this, Charlie?" His wizened face had a leathery look and his teeth were permanently stained from years of chewing tobacco, a habit Pete had given up due to his doctor's request and an aging, sensitive stomach. But one cheek bulged a little, as though it still contained a chaw.

The Dirksens and the McAllisters had been friends for as long as Charlie could remember. Pete and his wife, Mave, were the closest thing to family that Charlie and her sister, Cassie, had had since their father's death.

Charlie squared her shoulders. "I'm ready," she announced grimly. "How about you?"

"There's two blocks of timber up for bid today. If I don't get one of them, I'm done, Charlie."

Charlie had known Pete was getting close to the end, just as she was. But hearing it from the old man's lips made it worse. "Damn," she muttered, sending a dark frown across the room to Rick Slaughter's casually slouched figure. "Pete, if I manage to secure one of the blocks, I'll share it with you."

"Thanks, honey. But you need it as bad as me. No, I think I'm just about ready to throw in the towel. I've got a little money put aside, and me and Mave have been thinking of headin' south anyway. If I get one of the sales, fine. If I don't, that's it. That's where I stand."

Pete gave Charlie a sideways glance. She was no slip of a girl. Charlie McAllister was a strong young woman, a fine figure of a woman, really. But he felt awfully sorry for her right this minute. Butting heads with a company the size and scope of Canfield Lumber was something few men would want to take on. And despite the ability Charlie had exhibited in operating the family sawmill since Dave's death, she was still a woman. Pete sighed sadly, a little for himself, a lot for his younger companion.

For Charlie, Pete's sigh brought a curling anger, anger that Canfield's voracious timber appetite was very close to claiming another victim. And how much longer could she hang on? McAllister Lumber Company was very near the end, too. If she didn't get one of today's sales, she had maybe four weeks—six at the outside—of operating time left. Her log supply was dwindling daily, with no replacement in sight.

What would her father do if he were alive and well? It was a question Charlie asked herself often, and not just about the present situation. Dave McAllister had been one of the best small-mill operators in the country, and what he had taught Charlie lived on in her mind despite his being gone for six years now.

She was twenty years old and in college when her father had had his first stroke eight years earlier. Her sister, Cassie, had been just a kid, only twelve, and unable to assume the responsibility of an almost helpless father. Charlie had rushed home, and for two years she not only took care of a semi-invalid, but kept the sawmill going, too. During that time, even though Dave wasn't able to get down to the mill, his advice had been invaluable.

Charlie glanced at her watch. The sale was set for eleven and she knew it would begin promptly and last only a short time. Successful or not in the bidding, she'd promised to have lunch with Cassie before she left Missoula and drove the thirty miles back to Gibbs, the small town where both her home and the sawmill were located.

Cassie was another worry for Charlie. Their mother had died when Cassie was a mere toddler, and Charlie had grown up mothering her baby sister with a fiercely protective watchfulness. She still harbored a deep sense of responsibility for the younger woman and lived in dread of the day when the family business would no longer be able to help support Cassie's education. Charlie had no regrets about cutting her own education short at the age of twenty. She loved the lumber business unconditionally, accepting fluctuating markets and mechanical snafus without complaint. With sufficient timber, she would happily operate the sawmill on into a long, contented future. Cassie was of an entirely different nature.

Education was very important to Cassandra McAllister. The sawmill was only a mass of noisy equipment to her, perplexing and not interesting enough to delve into. Cassie wanted to teach—she'd always wanted to teach—and it was as important to Charlie as it was to Cassie that she attain her goal. Lately Charlie had been putting in some sleepless nights worrying about it.

One wouldn't know it by looking at her, though. Charlie exuded confidence whether she felt it or not. She was a strongly built woman with broad shoulders, a straight back and a full, high bosom. Her hips were firm and slender and her legs long and usually clad, as they were today, in blue denim. She had a remarkable face. It wasn't softly pretty as Cassie's was, but Charlie's features were every bit as nicely proportioned; and her smooth skin, high cheekbones and deep-set eyes conveyed a much more serious nature than Cassie's did.

Charlie's eyes had an unusual shading, somewhere between a gold and green, depending on mood. Anyone who really knew her also knew that her eyes were perfect indicators of what she was feeling, for when she was calm they radiated a golden light; when riled, they shot vivid green sparks.

The sisters' hair was very near the same color, a pale golden blond. But Cassie wore hers in a curly cap and Charlie preferred the stylish simplicity of one long French braid. She had originally adopted the style because it required very little fuss and kept her hair out of the way of machinery. With time, however, Charlie had become so used to her braid that she couldn't imagine doing anything else with her thick mane.

A side door opened and Jim Baker entered the room. Jim was the government forester who handled local timber sales, and he smiled and greeted the three attendees. "Well, this is it," Pete remarked in an undertone.

The procedure was simple. Jim read a description of the offering, which everyone was already familiar with from advance information, then asked for bids. Charlie wrote her figure on the appropriate form, as did Pete and Rick. Then Jim collected the bids. A second man came in, and together the two foresters checked the offers.

Canfield Lumber Company was promptly announced as the successful bidder, and Charlie and Pete exchanged emotionless glances. It went exactly the same for the second block of timber—Canfield topped both Charlie and Pete.

Pete stood up with an air of finality. "Well, I guess that's that. Heading right back, Charlie?"

"I'm meeting Cassie for lunch first. I'll walk out with you." Charlie picked up her brown leather shoulder bag, aware that the knot in her stomach would more than likely preclude any enjoyment of lunch.

Rick was talking to Jim when Charlie and Pete left, and the two of them exited the building and walked to the parking lot. Evidently Pete wasn't going to dwell on what had just taken place because he asked after Cassie.

"She's fine, Pete. Making excellent grades." They stopped alongside Charlie's blue pickup truck. The sun was warm, yet Charlie fought a chill. She could speak of other things, but she couldn't think about them. All that was in her mind was the past few minutes and how they had sealed her fate.

"How much longer will you operate?" Charlie asked with a taut expression.

Pete looked off into the distance. "It shouldn't take long to wrap things up. I don't know, maybe a few weeks."

"Then you and Mave will leave Gibbs?"

Pete nodded. "Been thinking about Arizona. The winters here are getting Mave down. Me, too, I guess. We're getting old, Charlie. Maybe it's best I didn't get one of those sales." The old man's eyes narrowed. "But you now, that's a different story. You're young and have a lot of years ahead of you. What will you do?"

Charlie shook her head slowly. "I honestly don't know," she answered quietly. "I thought I stood a good chance of getting one of the sales. I even bid a higher figure than I should have. Canfield's bid was ridiculously high."

Pete hitched up his jeans. "Sure was. Well, Morgan's managed to cook everyone's goose, hasn't he?"

Charlie knew full well who Morgan was, even if she hadn't met the man. Cole Morgan was a favorite topic of conversation and speculation around the Three Forks area, a rural community that encompassed a dozen or so ranches, Canfield Lumber Company and the town of Gibbs. Before Cole Morgan bought Canfield two years ago, the massive lumber and timber company had peacefully coexisted with the area's small sawmillers. It was only after Morgan assumed ownership that Charlie's timber problems had begun.

Oh, yes, she knew very well who Morgan was. Just the name could raise her hackles. "Have you met him, Pete?" she asked, wondering about the man who had altered so many lives.

"Yeah, I did. Shortly after he bought Canfield." Pete shrugged. "Seemed like a nice enough fellow. Never can tell, I guess."

"Yes," Charlie agreed soberly. "You never can tell. From what I've heard, he's finally moving to Montana."

"Have you seen the house he's having built on the Bitterroot River?"

"Can't say that I have," Charlie drawled dryly. "Have you?"

Pete nodded with a keen, bright light of amusement in his eyes. "It's quite a place, Charlie."

Charlie looked away, spotting Rick Slaughter coming out of the building. "Actually, I'm not overly interested in Cole Morgan's future home," she murmured, adding, "Here comes Rick."

"Never did like him. He's not from around here, you know," Pete said crustily, as though Rick's distant origins explained his self-centered personality.

The rather narrow opinion made Charlie smile in spite of her tension, and when Rick veered in their direction, he was inadvertently on the receiving end of that smile. At once he smiled back. "Nice day," he called out as he approached.

Charlie's countenance cooled, but she did manage a brief reply. "Very." Pete merely grunted.

Rick wasn't much taller than Charlie, but he was stockily built, with heavy shoulders and thighs, a thatch of dark hair and a reasonably handsome face. Charlie knew that Rick was considered something of a ladies' man around Gibbs, but she'd never understood why. He had an almost unctuous manner, varying it with degrees of superiority, which made him either distasteful or irritating. Add to those unredeeming qualities his habit of visually undressing her every time they met, and Charlie felt justified in being uneasy around the man.

Rick was in one of his overly obsequious moods. "Sorry you both lost in there," he said with an exaggeratedly chagrined expression.

Pete turned and spat, a gesture reminiscent of his tobacco-chewing days. Charlie regarded Rick through cool eyes. "I think we both expected it." She was silent a moment. "Pete will be shutting his mill down in a matter of weeks," she added, watching Rick's show of surprise in private amazement. Did he actually have the effrontery to pretend ignorance of the situation?

"Planning on retirement, Pete? Well, you're probably ready for it, huh?"

Pete gave the man a cynically amused look, but before he could make a reply, Charlie snapped, "I'm not."

Rick's head jerked around. "Hell no! You're in the prime of life." As though a survey were necessary backup to his observation, Rick's eyes traveled up and down Charlie's body.

She flushed despite a vow not to let it bother her. There was no point in bandying words with Rick. She was getting angry and apt to say something she'd regret later. Charlie turned to her old friend. "I've got to get going, Pete. Say hello to Mave for me and tell her I'll stop by in the next few days."

"I'll do that." Without so much as a glance at Rick, Pete walked over to his own pickup and got in.

Charlie pulled open the door of her truck and climbed up into the seat, aware that Rick still stood by. She slammed the door. The window was open, though, and she gave him a cool "Goodbye," certainly a whole lot more than Pete had offered.

Rick stepped to the window and peered in. "I sure would like to make this up to you, Charlie."

Charlie arched a dubious eyebrow. "And how would you propose to do that?"

A little-boy grin curved Rick's lips, the sort of grin that Charlie suspected the man thought was just too, too appealing to resist. "Dinner some evening? I'd sure like the opportunity to show you a good time."

It wasn't the first time Rick had declared a personal interest, but coming on top of the final blow to her professional life, Charlie felt her blood begin a slow boil. She lifted her chin at the same time she started the truck. "No, thanks, but I'll give you one thing, Rick. You've got more gall than any man I've ever known. With one blow this morning you put my old friend Pete and me both out of business, and you think you can mend fences by buying me dinner?"

"Hey, it's not my doing," Rick quickly denied, backing up with an innocent expression. "I'm only doing my job. Talk to my boss if you've got complaints."

"Cole Morgan?"

"You've got it. I'm only following his orders."

Charlie regarded Rick for a long, speculative moment. "You know, that's not such a bad idea." Slamming the truck into reverse, Charlie backed out of the parking space and drove away with only one very small satisfaction—the look on Rick's face. He hadn't appeared particularly happy that she might take him up on his suggestion to speak to his boss.

DURING THE DRIVE to the restaurant Charlie mulled it over. Why not speak to Cole Morgan? Unlike Pete, she wasn't ready to call it quits. In fact, she was a long way from willingly giving up a business her father had lived his life building. Morgan was in the area now, at least presenting the possibility for her to meet him, and perhaps "complaining," as Rick had so rudely put it, just might do some good.

Cassie was already at the restaurant, seated in a booth, when Charlie arrived. She stood up and hugged her sister. "How'd the sale go?"

They sat down and Charlie shook her head. "Not good. Canfield got both blocks of timber."

Through lovely blue-gray eyes Cassie regarded her sister sadly. "What are you going to do?"

"I'm not sure." Charlie picked up a menu, quickly scanned the items listed and closed it again. "Actually, Rick Slaughter squirmed out of any responsibility by telling me he was only doing his job and I should do my complaining to his boss. I've been giving it some thought."

"Do you think it would help?"

Charlie shrugged. "Who knows? I suppose it depends on what kind of man Cole Morgan is."

"Surely he knows what's been going on, doesn't he?"

"Good question," Charlie muttered, then raised an inquiring eyebrow. "Does it seem possible he wouldn't? I mean, even an absentee owner has to keep abreast of what's going on outside the immediate operation of his own business, doesn't he?"

Cassie nodded. "I would think so."

"He's been in and out of the area periodically. Word gets around." Charlie sighed. "He has to know. How can I think otherwise? Besides, from what Rick said, Morgan's the man giving the orders."

"You and Pete are the only small-mill operators still running in western Montana," Cassie said softly, sympathetically.

"Only me after a few more weeks. Pete's quitting, too."

"Oh, Charlie, really?"

"He and Mave are planning to move south. I guess I can't blame them, Cass. They're not young anymore, and Pete said they have a little money saved. I think he's just plain tired of fighting the battle."

"Is he going to sell his mill?"

Charlie smirked. "Who'd buy it without timber? That's the same boat you and I are in, Cass. The mill represents a lot of money, but without timber it's just so much cold steel."

Cassie grew thoughtful. "We still have that section of land Dad bought years ago. It must be worth something."

"It was worth quite a lot until I took all the good timber off it. We discussed it, Cassie. Without that timber I would have been out of business a year ago."

"I know. I'm not faulting what you did, Charlie. All I'm trying to do is help you out of this mess." Cassie leaned forward. "Just chuck the whole thing, sis. Come back to school and get your degree. We could share an apartment and—"

"Not yet, Cassie. I'm not giving up that easily."

Her sister's determined expression forestalled further suggestions of this type. Cassie well knew Charlie's obsession with the lumber business even if she didn't understand it. Still, it was Charlie who kept the two of them going, although Cassie had been giving that a lot of thought lately. She had a few ideas, but didn't want to mention them until they were more concrete. "Let's order lunch," she said quietly.

IN THE DAYS THAT FOLLOWED, seeking out Cole Morgan diminished in urgency as Charlie dealt with several emergencies. First, a sizable and crucial electric motor gave out in the mill, necessitating a rush trip to Missoula. The next day, with the mill running again, one of the crewmen was injured when a long splinter flew from a board and embedded itself in his arm. It took the remainder of that afternoon to drive the young man to Missoula for medical attention.

By Friday it seemed that the week had consisted mainly of trips to Missoula. Some weeks seemed to go that way, Charlie knew, and wasn't daunted by it. However, her absences from the office had created a backlog of paperwork. The company's longtime secretary had recently quit because of her husband's employment transfer, and with the future so shaky, Charlie hadn't even attempted to replace her.

Settled at her desk, Charlie waded through the payroll, which had to be out by quitting time that day, then turned to some invoicing. Deeply enmeshed in the complexities of lumber footages, she didn't notice when someone came in. Her office was the second room in the small, two-room building, and from her desk she couldn't see the front door. It wasn't until a masculine voice boomed "Anybody here?" that Charlie realized she was no longer alone.

She jumped up, rounded her desk and called at the same time, "Yes, I'm coming." Charlie stopped in the doorway, then advanced into the other room with less speed. "Hello."

A big man brought his wandering gaze to her, then smiled. "Hi. I was beginning to think the place was deserted."

The man created quite an impact. In one overwhelming moment Charlie took in incredibly broad shoulders in a well-cut white shirt, a flat-as-a-board belly, snug-fitting jeans and a smile that could probably melt the polar cap. With dark, unruly hair laced with silvery strands, heavy eyebrows over piercing blue eyes, a craggy jaw and a wide mouth that immediately made her think the word "sexy," this stranger was the sort of rare male most women only dreamed of meeting. And he had walked into *her* office.

Charlie took another step forward. "I'm afraid I was too involved to hear you come in."

"Quite all right. I'm trying to meet my neighbors. Is the owner around?"

"The owner?" Charlie couldn't resist an amused smile. "You're looking at her."

"I am? You're *Charlie* McAllister?" The question was accompanied by a puzzled frown. "But . . ."

Charlie walked over to the vacant desk in a corner of the room and sat on the edge of it. "Actually, it's pronounced 'Sharlie,' short for Charlotte. Or, it used to be. I think the people around here have probably forgotten I was christened Charlotte."

"And you run this mill. Well, I guess you're the one I came to meet then. I'm Cole Morgan." Cole stepped closer and extended his hand.

If the man had suddenly kicked her in the shin, Charlie couldn't have been more startled. She jerked away from the desk in an awkward rush and stood up straight, aware of a terrible disappointment. This handsome hunk of masculinity was Cole Morgan, her and every other local sawmiller's nemesis!

Cole's frown reappeared. Wasn't she going to shake his hand? She certainly wasn't what he'd expected. No one had told him Charlie McAllister was a woman. But even if they had, he wouldn't have anticipated her being one with pale golden hair, a knockout figure and, yes, gorgeous green eyes.

But there was a very strange look in that radiant green, and Cole didn't know what to make of it. He almost dropped his hand, feeling somewhat foolish with it stuck out in midair, but Charlie suddenly took it. The contact was warm and oddly exciting . . . and brief.

She turned away, trying to remember what she'd wanted to tell this man. Complaining in her mind to a faceless image was one thing, baring her timberless soul to this ruggedly handsome individual, quite another. He was speaking, and Charlie spun around.

"I hope you'll accept my apologies, Charlie. I should have made this call long ago. Other business interests kept me away, but I've cleaned everything else up and intend making my home here now."

"I heard you were building a house out on the river." *My Lord, his eyes are blue!* She also noticed that Cole Morgan's skin was just tan enough and his teeth were a startling white.

Cole took a small notebook from his shirt pocket and thumbed through it. "I'd enjoy seeing your operation, if you don't mind. Then . . ." He read from the notebook. "I intend stopping in at the other mills in the area. Lester Mann—"

"Lester's mill is closed."

"Well, there are four others here."

"All closed. Except Pete Dirksen's. It will be closed in two weeks." Charlie relayed the information without emotion, although curiosity was developing at Morgan's apparently outdated facts.

But perhaps the man was a consummate actor. How could he not know what had happened to the lumber industry in western Montana since his purchase of Canfield? As she'd wondered to Cassie, was it even possible Morgan didn't know? Charlie grew wary, suspecting this man of playing a rather cruel game.

"All closed?" Cole's brow knit thoughtfully. "That's odd. Two years ago—"

"Two years ago there were six small mills operating within a thirty-mile radius," Charlie confirmed with a cautious nod. "Today there are two. By fall there won't be any. Rather clears the field of competition, doesn't it?"

Cole gave her a perplexed look as he tried to grasp the meaning behind what sounded like an accusation. "I'm not sure I understand. Are you intimating I should be more aware? I can't disagree with that, but as I said, I haven't been able to spend much time here."

He seemed so sincere, and like Pete had acclaimed, a pretty nice guy. But, as they'd both agreed, one couldn't always tell. "I'm not intimating anything," Charlie said quietly, deciding to back off . . . for the moment.

Cole Morgan's desire to see her operation wasn't unusual, even though it was somewhat tardy. Sawmillers were notorious for snooping around each other's operations, probably because they shared a love for an industry that outsiders couldn't begin to grasp. Many times strangers passing through the area stopped, introduced themselves and asked to tour the plant.

Charlie hung on to that thought and managed to maintain a civil expression. "Feel free to inspect the mill if you want to. I have no objection."

"Thanks, I will." Cole started for the door, then turned. "But before I go, would you mind telling me why you're planning to shut down before fall?"

There wasn't an ounce of emotion on Charlie's face, yet every cell in her body had leaped at the man's gall. For a moment she teetered between launching an out-and-out assault on the cause of all her problems and maintaining a hold on some sort of dignity. Dignity won, but only to a point. Her voice was controlled, but her fingernails were digging into her palms when she said, "On your way to the mill, take a look at my log yard, Mr. Morgan. I'm sure that will answer your question quite clearly."

2

STRUGGLING FOR OBJECTIVITY, Charlie peered out a back window as Cole walked the distance between the office and mill. He had a long-legged stride that she watched with a critical eye, unable to detect even a tiny flaw in his narrow hips and muscular legs. He wore Western boots, much like her own, and the long sleeves of his shirt were rolled up to about midforearm, revealing powerful-looking wrists.

That's what she'd picked up from him, Charlie realized, a feeling of power, a strong sense of self. Yes, he had a "nice guy" facade, but certainly it had to be a deceptive front. Running a business long-distance might preclude knowing everything that went on in a community, but Morgan had been in the area often enough to be better informed that he'd said. It had to be an act.

Charlie's eyes narrowed as she watched him stop at the log yard. For several minutes he scanned the pitifully few logs, and even with the distance between them she could see perplexity in his stance.

"Good act," she muttered, unwilling to give Cole Morgan the benefit of the doubt. She couldn't be that generous, not when she was facing a shutdown that his ethics, or lack thereof, had caused.

He was outrageously attractive, wasn't he?

The unbidden thought made Charlie wince. A handsome face and strong body weren't going to influence her judgment, not if she had anything to say about it. Men were no big mystery, even those rare individuals with Cole Morgan's abundant physical assets. Charlie accepted and dealt with her own sexuality as she did other aspects of her life: honestly and directly. There'd been men, not a long list, but a few who had meant something for a while.

There'd always been something missing in those relationships, however, an element she'd never quite succeeded in putting a name to. She did suspect it had to do with what she did for a living, work that seemed to either awe or embarrass a man. She knew she projected strength, that was her way. But putting personality aside, she would apologize to no one for her career preference, and often Charlie had sensed withdrawal once a man understood that.

Charlie knew it would take a strong, secure man to accept her as she was. She thought of that again while watching Cole Morgan's meandering path to the mill, and it struck her that Canfield's owner seemed secure enough to deal with just about anything, even an iron-willed woman like herself.

The thought shocked her away from the window. She had spent no more than five minutes in Cole Morgan's company and she could hardly believe where some completely unsolicited imagery had taken her. Thinking of Morgan as anything but what he was, the man behind her business's impending demise, and several others', as well, was only asking for trouble, which she already had quite enough of.

Determinedly Charlie marched back to her own office. She had a deskful of work to do, and spying on Cole Morgan was just plain silly anyway.

The minutes passed while Charlie forced her mind on her work. A strange disappointment kept her from complete concentration, however, and finally, after making several mistakes and corrections, she sat back and toyed with the pencil she'd been using. She might as well admit she'd been impressed with Cole Morgan at first sight and disappointed after learning who he was. That wasn't a crime. How often did a man with his obvious physical attributes walk into one's life? No, it wasn't a crime to admire a handsome man. If there was any crime in the situation, it was in his being the man behind Rick Slaughter, the man "giving the orders," as Rick had stated so defensively.

Charlie got up, poured herself a cup of stale coffee from the hours-old pot and wandered back to the other room. At the window again, she sipped the strong brew and watched the mill building.

Even here in the office the screech of machinery was clearly audible, but it was music to Charlie's ears. She was so in tune with the mill's equipment, she could tell just by its sound if everything was running right. At the moment the mill was going full blast, and in her mind's eye she could visualize her fifteen crewmen's various activities. It was satisfying to know that Cole Morgan was seeing her operation at its best. Whatever he might have expected to see at McAllister Lumber Company, he was seeing a small but efficiently run, productive plant.

Charlie spotted Cole coming through one of the several mill doors and stiffened involuntarily. He was still looking, she could see, right now through the stacks of lumber awaiting shipment.

In a few minutes he started back in the direction of the office. Charlie moved away from the window and returned to her desk. The last thing she wanted was for Morgan to think she was the least bit shook over his visit. If he decided to come into the office again, he would find her knee deep in paperwork, as she should be.

Her heart thudded alarmingly while she listened for footfalls, though. It was a beat in her chest Charlie was all too aware of, but only because of who he was, she told herself firmly, not because he had thick dark hair and vivid blue eyes.

Although she was half expecting the sound, Charlie jumped as heavy boots trod the wood walkway and entered the office. She got up slowly, hearing no falter in the footsteps as they grew louder. Cole appeared in the doorway. He looked sober, thoughtful. "You've got a nice little plant here, Charlie. And I did take a look at your log yard. What's going on?"

Charlie couldn't believe he didn't know the answer to that as well as she did. She felt a wave of resentment heighten her color. "I'm out of timber," she said tersely, adding mentally, *As you well know!*

A snort preceded Cole's "How could anyone be out of timber around here? This is one of the best timber areas in the country."

He had the nerve to tell her that? She'd been born and raised in western Montana, and sure didn't need a relative newcomer explaining the abundance of local timber to her. Charlie's chin came up. "Really? Perhaps your observation would be of some comfort to Lester Mann. Or Pete Dirksen. I really can't speak for them, or for the other small-mill owners who've had to stop operating. But for my part, the fact that these mountains are loaded with trees doesn't make me particularly secure, not when I haven't been able to buy one stick for two years."

Cole's eyes narrowed and he stepped farther into the small room. "Why not?"

Was he serious? Charlie felt a ridiculous urge to laugh and stifled it with a rather impolite smirk.

The desk was between them, and on Cole's side, two chairs resided. He placed his hands on the back of one and leaned forward. "Why haven't you been able to buy any timber?" he repeated softly.

Should she be truthful? Hedge? The man was intimidating, in size, in demeanor. There was a strange, dark light in his eyes, as if he suspected the answer and was only waiting for confirmation. But that was silly. Of course he knew the answer. He'd caused the whole mess in the first place. Why should she worry about saying the right thing? She was the victim here and entitled to honesty.

Still, the breath Charlie drew sounded shaky. She had to force the words out. "Because I haven't been able to outbid Canfield."

Cole never moved. He just kept staring at her. "And the other mills?"

"The same thing."

"So, what you're telling me is that I've brought about the ruination of . . . how many mills, Charlie?"

"Uh . . . I'd rather not say," she stammered, reluctant to be quite that accusing. Not all of the small mill owners now out of business had been good operators.

Cole was silent a moment, although his gaze never wavered. As the recipient of such intense scrutiny, Charlie was growing uncomfortable. She was hemmed in and beginning to feel claustrophobic. With the bulk of Cole Morgan blocking her route to the door, and the office oddly dwarfed by his personality and size, it was little wonder, she acknowledged nervously.

Cole's silence stretched as he thought about Charlie's plight. He didn't know her, and maybe she was merely a loser looking for a scapegoat. Maybe not above making a little trouble if it suited her purpose, either. Just because she was one sensational-looking woman didn't mean she wasn't a troublemaker.

But what about those other mills? Was there a grain of truth in her accusation?

Frowning, Cole stood away from the chair. "I take it you're talking about federal timber. What about private stock?"

Charlie's shrug contained some relief. If the man was playacting, he was doing a darn good job of it, and despite his exalted position in the lumber business, there was a slim chance he wasn't completely aware of local conditions. "There's never much private timber on the market," she relayed with less tension. "Not unless you're prepared to buy land, too. Ranchers sell a little timber now and then, but it's not a steady supply."

"Besides," she added with a little more force, "anything of any size that was offered by the private sector in the past two years was snapped up by Rick Slaughter."

Cole rubbed his jaw reflectively. "Well, that's what I hired him for. When I took Canfield over it was dangerously short of timber. Rick's only doing his job."

"So he said," Charlie stated dryly.

"Then you've discussed this with Rick?" Curiosity blazed in the bluest eyes Charlie had ever seen.

"Discussed it?" Now Charlie did hedge. Had she ever attempted a real discussion of the problem with Rick? Most of the time the man irritated her so much, it was difficult to even maintain civility in his presence. Yet she knew Rick was totally aware of what had been happening with the small sawmillers. It was on his face and in his unctuous manner every time she saw him. He would have to be deaf, dumb, blind and stupid not to know, and Rick Slaughter might be unbearably irritating, but he wasn't any of those things.

How could she explain to Cole Morgan that his timber supervisor unnerved her so much with his leering, insulting looks that she hadn't even thought of confronting him with a frank, straightforward discussion? Charlie's heart sank; she was definitely guilty of letting a personal dislike get in the way of business, something she hadn't realized before, nor even thought herself impractical enough to do. It loomed as a terrible oversight with Cole Morgan's piercing blue eyes on her, one that she could barely tolerate admitting to herself, let alone blurt out in a self-condemning confession.

"Rick knows," she said lamely, averting her gaze, bringing it down to the array of papers on the desk. She felt at a loss standing behind the desk with Morgan pinning her down. The man was overwhelming, bright, articulate . . . and too damned good-looking. He disturbed Charlie in a way she'd never been disturbed before. It was that air of authority he emanated, along with too much rugged, macho appeal that made her feel at a disadvantage, she decided. Best end this question-and-answer session right now.

"I really have a lot of paperwork to get done . . ." She left the sentence dangling, hoping he would take the hint.

Cole's eyes flicked to the desk, then back to her face. Pretty. No, not pretty. Beautiful. Beautiful in an arresting, interesting way. Her hair and eye color were exceptional, and her skin looked utterly poreless, like creamy satin. No makeup, a strange sophistication in that hairstyle, a body starlets would kill for, long legs. . . God, the local men must be beating her door down.

Was she involved with anyone? Was she married? She wore no jewelry other than a rather masculine-looking watch, but that wasn't proof. Yet, wouldn't a husband be a visible part of the operation? In fact, why was she in this office all alone? No one could run a mill and do all the paperwork by themselves.

Cole couldn't resist. He had to ask. "Don't you have any help in here?"

"I did. My secretary left the area last month."

"And you've been handling the mill *and* the paperwork? What are you—some kind of superwoman?"

A flush seared Charlie's face. How dare he ridicule her efforts? She wouldn't be in this untenable situation if he weren't so damned greedy! "I hardly need your approval, Mr. Morgan."

"I wasn't disapproving, Charlie. I'm impressed."

"Oh. Well, I'm sorry if I misinterpreted your sarcasm. Now, if you'll excuse me . . ."

It hit Cole that Charlotte McAllister didn't like him. She chose to give the worst possible interpretation to his words, almost as if she was determined to maintain a breach between them. Obviously she'd had her mind made up about him before this meeting, and little he could say or do would alter that opinion.

Too bad. He would have liked to get to know Charlie better. He had never expected to meet someone like her in a sawmill. It was a rare woman who understood what the lumber business could mean to a man; it wasn't just a profession, it was a consuming, incredibly satisfying way of life.

Cole nodded. "I'll let you get back to work. Nice meeting you, Charlie."

"Thank you," she replied stiffly.

Cole walked to the door, then turned with a faint grin. "It wasn't nice meeting me, though, was it?"

Charlie's pulse jumped erratically as she felt her cheeks flush again. "It was nice of you to stop by. Thank you."

A small chuckle preceded "Well, you're tactful. I'll give you that. So long, Charlie. See you around."

Charlie sank into her chair as the sound of Cole's foot-steps resounded through the office. In a moment she heard his pickup start up and drive away, and when she couldn't detect it any longer, she released a long, tremulous breath, realizing she was sitting tensely on the edge of the chair.

Cole Morgan had made quite an impression, but it was one Charlie found impossible to sort out. She wasn't sure, even after thinking about it long and hard, whether she was more impressed with his confident manner or with his vivid blue eyes and the fit of his jeans.

Being almost girlishly impressed with masculine good looks wasn't something she was overly pleased with, however, especially when the object of her admiration was a man she should only dislike.

Well, it probably didn't matter one way or the other. Their paths weren't apt to cross again, even if she managed to keep operating. The spectrum of lumbering encompassed vast opposites, with enormous companies on one end and tiny one- and two-man operations on the other. Canfield hovered somewhere near the top of the scale and McAllister Lumber Company occupied a spot very near the bottom. Only monetarily speaking, of course. It was impossible to put a dollars-and-cents value on emotional involvement, and Charlie would put her lifetime of love and caring for the lumber industry up against Morgan's any day.

That was beside the point, though. It was the disparity in size and success of the operations that made Charlie feel she and Cole Morgan would see little of each other. Oh, she would be welcome to tour his plant, just as she had allowed him to inspect hers. That was a courtesy mill owners extended to one another. Once past that, however, if sawmillers had no other common ground, they didn't automatically become friends.

No, it was highly unlikely she would run into Cole very often. With his lofty position in the community, he would no doubt hobnob with the larger ranchers and businessmen and women from Missoula. Charlie's friends were lifelong, people she grew up with—couples like Pete and Mave Dirksen, old friends of her father, none of whom were apt to draw Cole Morgan's notice.

It was probably for the best. Running into Mr. Morgan when she had such conflicting feelings about him wasn't something she, nor any other thinking woman, would want. There was really only one good thing about his dropping in so unexpectedly: she had finally met the man behind Rick Slaughter, and the man who was the topic of so many conversations around Gibbs.

At least now she had a face to attach to the Morgan name.

THE SPRING TERM was finally over at the university in Missoula, and Charlie expected her sister to come home for a few weeks, until Cassie would take the summer class she had mentioned a few months before. However, instead of Cassie bursting in with luggage and a big hug, Charlie got a phone call.

"I've got a job with a bank, sis," Cassie cheerfully related.

Charlie became immediately suspicious. "Just for the summer?"

"Of course," Cassie replied without hesitation.

"I thought you were signed up for a summer class."

"It's nothing I can't take later. This job just sort of fell into my lap. It's good pay and I really want to do it."

Charlie was far from convinced. Deep down she knew what Cassie was doing: trying to make her older sister's financial load easier. It touched Charlie but also upset her. If she remembered the conversation correctly when Cassie originally spoke of the summer class, she had declared it to be a special course she couldn't get during the fall term.

Still, Charlie knew she was in no position to object. Three months of a well-paying job would help a lot with fall tuition. And by then she might be looking for a job herself. "All right, Cass," she sighed. "I understand. Can you come home for the weekend?"

"I'm afraid not." Cassie laughed. "I'll be working at the bookstore. Luke was kind enough to rearrange my hours so I could handle both jobs. Isn't that great?"

"Yeah, great," Charlie said dryly, fighting a surge of bitterness. Cassie's part-time job at the bookstore had originally been needed only as a supplement to Charlie's support. In the past, the ten to twenty hours a week Cassie put in had taken care of extras. Now . . .

"I'm not very thrilled about this," Charlie said wearily.

"Sis, you're doing everything you can for the two of us. You've got to allow me the same latitude."

Charlie was so used to mothering her sister that Cassie's softly stated plea took her by surprise. Cassie wasn't a child anymore and hadn't been for a long time, Charlie suddenly realized, even if she had continued to see her in that light. Now, when the McAllister family's finances were becoming very slim indeed, Cassie wanted to do her part. Charlie felt the sting of tears, recognizing the same spirit in her sister that she'd inherited from their father. Dave's determination was in them both, perhaps not quite to the same extent in Cassie, but it was there just the same, urging them to fight and kick when the chips were down.

When the conversation was over, Charlie vowed with even more intensity to work her way out of this quandary. There had to be a solution, and come hell or high water, she was going to find it!

That weekend Charlie hit the road. The mill never ran on Saturday unless a breakdown during the week demanded to be made up for. With all that free time on her hands, she could start making the rounds of local ranches early Saturday morning. It was ground she had covered before, but undaunted, she drove dusty ranch roads and knocked on doors to inquire about timber.

Saturday proved fruitless other than for seeing some old friends who were thrilled she dropped in. Sunday morning she ran across a rancher who wanted to clear twenty acres of trees to put in an alfalfa crop, but the trees were sparse and would offer only another two weeks' operation for the mill. Every little bit helped, though, Charlie determined, and she gratefully made the necessary arrangements to log the man's property.

By Sunday afternoon she was driving back to Gibbs feeling pretty disheartened. Other than two ranches where she hadn't found anyone home, she'd covered the area. The sun was warm and she drove with the pickup's windows down, enjoying the lovely breezes ruffling strands of hair from her braid.

It dawned on her that she was on the Bitterroot River road, after having taken a circuitous route back to town, and she couldn't help watching for the house Cole Morgan was having built out there. When she spotted it, she was amazed. Certainly as spectacular as gossip claimed it to be, the large, natural cedar structure was nearing completion on a bluff above the river. It must have an exceptional view, she mused.

Adorned with tinted windows clear across the front of the house, two massive rock chimneys and an enormous shake roof, the place promised to be magnificent when finished, and the choice of building materials fit in beautifully with its environment of tall pine and fir trees.

The house was quite a way from the road, and Charlie drove past it very slowly, admiring it from every angle. Oddly, it was rather easy to place Cole Morgan in such a house. His size demanded space, and his strong personality seemed to match the rugged lines of sloping room and sternly forested surroundings.

Feeling she was getting entirely too poetic with an unfinished house and a man she hardly knew, Charlie laughed at herself and stepped on the accelerator. She might as well go home and—

With a jolt and a wobble the pickup lurched to the right. A flat tire! "Dammit!" Charlie cried, gripping the steering wheel tighter and easing up on the gas. She managed to steer the truck to the side of the road without mishap, then turned off the ignition with another "Damn!" The prospect of changing a tire was an irritation at a time when she didn't need any.

She slammed the door behind her with more force than necessary and walked around the back of the pickup to inspect the damage. The right rear tire was flat, all right—the wheel was sitting right on the ground.

For a minute Charlie gave in to disgust and frustration. What else could go wrong? But seething by the side of the road ten miles from home wasn't going to get that tire changed, so she began to loosen the spare from its rack.

Charlie didn't look for help. She was perfectly capable of changing a tire, and she waved on by the few cars that slowed down questioningly. Traffic was light at best, with a vehicle passing only now and then. It took only a short time to roll the spare to the back of the truck and get the jack and lug wrench.

She was on her knees, struggling with a rusty, stubborn wheel bolt, when she heard another car approaching. Without looking up, she waved it on, but when it stopped only a few feet from the rear bumper of the truck, she glanced up to see the distinctive square nose of a black Lincoln.

She rose slowly, prepared to thank the driver for his concern and send him on his way. But words suddenly escaped her. Climbing out of the Lincoln, looking outrageously handsome in a dark suit, white shirt and sedate, deep red necktie, was Cole Morgan!

"Hello, Charlie. Got a problem here?" The door to the Lincoln closed with a heavy thud and Cole stepped forward.

For a moment Charlie was so flustered she was tongue-tied. Of all the rotten luck, this could be the all-time ultimate! A flat tire, a mulish wheel bolt, sweat on her face from wrestling with the spare and lug wrench, and this man comes along looking like a movie star!

Did she deserve this? God, did any woman deserve such a cruel twist of fate? Charlie let out an exasperated sigh and stated as calmly as she could manage, "It's only a flat tire. I can handle it just fine."

Cole took her in with one swooping glance. Her face was slightly flushed—no doubt from her efforts in the warm sun—but she was as striking as he remembered. Charlie had the kind of figure jeans were invented for, he thought with a touch of amused admiration, long legs, slender hips, small waist. And that emerald-green knit top she was wearing curved around a bustline that was pretty damned arousing. Yes, she was some special-looking woman, no two ways about it. "Let me give you a hand," he offered.

Charlie's gaze studied the sharp crease in his pant legs and the snowy white of his shirtfront. "Dressed like that?"

Laughing easily, Cole pulled the suit jacket off and folded it over the side of the pickup bed. "Don't worry. I won't get dirty, Mother."

Charlie had to laugh, too. But she really didn't need him to risk soiling his clothes—except maybe for a little assistance with that one wheel bolt. "Just do one thing," she asked. "There's one bolt I'm having trouble with."

"Sure...anything." Cole stooped down beside the tire and gave it a good look. He held up his hand for the lug wrench Charlie was hanging on to, and she passed it to him, having a hard time with the breadth of his shoulders in that white shirt. The men around Gibbs didn't dress so formally unless there was a special occasion, and Cole's attire was unusual for a Sunday afternoon. Was there anything more becoming to a man than a dark suit and white shirt? Oh, the fad clothes were great, but a dark suit gave a man stature . . . and mystery.

One pull from Cole was all it took to loosen the bolt, but he didn't stop at that. Charlie sighed, realizing the futility of telling him again she could finish the job herself. She stood back silently, wincing at the black rubber stains he was getting on his hands.

When the spare was securely in place, Cole stood up. "There, all finished."

"Thank you" was all Charlie could manage. She should despise this handsome man—but she didn't—and disloyalty to herself and all she and her father had worked for broiled within her.

Cole took out a spotless white handkerchief and wiped his hands. "I'm glad I ran into you, Charlie. I was going to call you anyway."

Her eyes widened. "You were?"

"Yes. I've got a business proposition to talk over with you. Sorry I don't have time right now. I'm on my way to Missoula for a meeting, but I could stop by your house this evening. Would that be all right?"

"I—I suppose so." A business proposition? What kind of business proposition? Charlie battled with mistrust, with suspicion, while Cole did the best he could with a dry handkerchief.

He grinned. "I'll have to stop somewhere and wash my hands."

"I knew you'd get dirty," she said absently, too enmeshed in the thought of this man coming to her house tonight to be concerned with his stained hands any longer.

"No problem," he declared, retrieving his jacket from the truck. "Where do you live, Charlie?"

Her thoughts suddenly returned from the fearful future to the uncomfortable present, and without enthusiasm she gave him directions.

"Good enough. I'll see you this evening."

Numbly Charlie watched him walk to his car, but she got her wits together enough to call, "Thanks again," just before he got in. After the Lincoln pulled around the truck and purred out of sight, she sighed wearily. Now, how was she going to deal with him this evening?

She really shouldn't even allow him in her house. She should meet him at the door and say, "You're not welcome here, Cole Morgan. After the havoc you've wreaked in this area, you're not welcome in anyone's home."

But it probably wasn't true. Anyone in Gibbs would no doubt trip over their own feet in opening the door for him.

Well, he *was* a nice guy. He'd proved that by stopping when he really shouldn't have, not dressed the way he was.

So, how come a nice guy had run people out of business?

What was Cole Morgan, a Dr. Jekyll and Mr. Hyde?

3

BY THE TIME CHARLIE had finished her simple supper, tidied the kitchen and gotten ready for Cole's arrival, she had pretty much convinced herself to remain uninvolved in whatever his "business proposition" might entail. She dared not trust him, she felt, and it galled her no end to know she'd have had no trouble with that if Canfield's owner hadn't been so tall, dark and handsome. Why good looks should influence common sense in the matter was uncomfortably puzzling, but they did. If Morgan had looked like a greedy, heartless mill owner—a caricatural image Charlie couldn't help smiling over—she wouldn't have had the slightest problem in dealing with him.

As it was, well... She chose a peach gauze dress for the evening rather than greet him in jeans.

Even to Charlie it seemed rather droll that she'd want to look her best when he came to her door and still, at the same time, understand the importance of keeping him at a safe business distance.

But perhaps the diverse attitudes weren't that unusual, she told herself as she put the finishing touches to her makeup. It was natural for a woman to feel more comfortable with an attractive man if she looked good, too, even to do business with him.

At eight Charlie put on a fresh pot of coffee, and to fill the vacant atmosphere of the house, turned on the stereo. The music helped to soothe the bad case of nerves she was developing, but her own ambivalent feelings toward Cole

Morgan would not allow her to take his visit lightly. On one hand he seemed much too nice to fit the villainous role she had cast him in prior to their initial meeting, but on the other hand, she couldn't diminish the seriousness of her situation, a situation she wouldn't be in if Canfield hadn't hogged all the government timber sales.

When she finally heard a car pull into the driveway, Charlie felt tremendous relief. She had reached the point of wanting to get this over with and went to the door at the first sound of a knock.

Cole was glancing around her yard when she opened the door, positively glorious in his casual pose on her front porch. He smiled that fabulous smile of his and by way of a greeting said, "Nice place, Charlie."

Charlie's heart pounded madly before it settled down and she could speak normally. That's what unnerved her around this man—how her own body could react so completely on its own. Where was her usual control, her self-assurance?

"Thank you. Please come in." She stood back with her hand on the doorknob, and Cole stepped across the threshold.

She brought him to the living room and walked over to switch off the stereo. "Would you like some coffee? There's a fresh pot."

"Yes, I would. Thanks." Cole stood in the center of the room.

"Please sit down," Charlie invited. "I'll only be a minute."

Cole watched her go to the kitchen, very aware of the peach dress and subtle makeup she was wearing. Had she done that for him? It pleased him that she might have taken the time to look especially nice for the meeting, and he read it as a good sign.

"Cream and sugar?" came from the kitchen.

"No, thanks," Cole called back. "Just black for me." He waited until she returned with a small tray and handed him one of the cups and saucers. When she was seated in a blue wing chair, he sat on the sofa. "Sorry I didn't get here sooner," he said after a sip of hot coffee. "The meeting lasted through dinner, which I hadn't expected."

"Quite all right," Charlie murmured, knowing now why she had made coffee. It gave her something to do with her hands. Gratefully, she raised the cup to her lips.

Cole's eyes swept the comfortably furnished room. "Do you live here alone?"

"Yes. My sister lives in Missoula. Our parents are dead."

"Sorry," Cole said quietly. "Mine are, too. I have two brothers and a sister, though. They all live in Oregon."

"Oh? Is that where you're from?"

Cole nodded. "Grants Pass, Oregon. Ever been there?"

"I've heard of it," Charlie replied. "But no, I've never been there."

"Pretty country. Oregon's a beautiful state."

Charlie met his blue-eyed gaze. "I'm sure it is. How did you get from there to Montana?"

Cole laughed, put his cup and saucer on the coffee table and leaned back with his arms stretched along the top of the sofa. His jacket gapped, allowing a good view of his trim waistline . . . which Charlie didn't miss. In fact, she was missing very few details about Cole Morgan, admiring again the cut of his excellent clothing and how relaxed his catlike movements were.

"Via Idaho, Alaska and Northern California, that's how," Cole declared, focusing Charlie's wandering thoughts on the common denominator of all the locales he'd mentioned.

"Those are all good timber states," she murmured.

"Exactly. I went from mill to mill, actually, upgrading a little each time. Canfield's the biggest operation I've had so far."

Instantly Charlie tensed. She was forgetting who and what Cole represented, allowing herself to become almost mesmerized by his impressive presence. Her comment was stammered, but heartfelt. "Canfield's . . . big, all right."

A pall had descended on their tentative camaraderie, and Cole brought his arms down, recognizing that Canfield's name had brought about the change. "Well, I suppose you're wondering what this is all about."

Charlie nodded, glad to be getting to the reason for this strange evening. "I'm curious, yes," she admitted.

"It's a simple proposition, Charlie. I'd like you to cut my small logs in your mill."

Charlie froze. She knew she was doing it, but nothing on God's green earth could have altered her reaction. "I beg your pardon?" she said in a hollow, disbelieving voice.

Cole leaned forward. "It would be a good arrangement for both of us, Charlie. Canfield operates most efficiently with large logs, and I've been thinking about putting in a small-log head rig, anyway. You'd have all the timber you wanted to cut and—"

"But I'd be working for you," she interrupted sharply.

"Well, yes, in a manner of speaking."

Perhaps one of the most satisfying aspects of operating McAllister Lumber Company was owner independence. Charlie hadn't had to answer to anyone since she took over. She ran her mill as she wanted to, sold her lumber to favored buyers, directed her crew without anyone else's influence or interference. In the blink of an eye Cole Morgan had created an image that gave her a disturbing sense of subservience. Even with an unknown face at the helm, the idea would be hard to swallow, but with Cole in the picture it was doubly unpalatable.

Answering to the man who had caused her problems in the first place, obeying his orders, doing his bidding, was a future that Charlie could hardly bear thinking about. Yet, dammit, it was an alternative to closing her doors!

He had her over the proverbial barrel, didn't he?

Charlie stirred angrily, got up and put her cup and saucer on a nearby table and walked over to the fireplace. Irrationally she took the time to wish she had her jeans and boots on. Why had she bothered with femininity? The man was as crass as she'd originally thought. His good looks were nothing but a deceptive front.

Cole rose slowly, a frown drawing his heavy brows together. He felt locked out of Charlie's thoughts, but it was pretty apparent she wasn't thrilled with the offer. "It didn't set right, did it?" he asked softly.

Charlie turned. Her features looked pinched and her eyes were a deep, sparky green. "Did you really think it would?"

"Yes. Yes, I did. I thought you'd welcome a way to keep operating. You'd make good money in the bargain."

Undergoing a strange loss of strength and a burning anger simultaneously gave Charlie's face a pale cast. "Let me make you an offer," she said tonelessly. "Get rid of those small logs slowing your plant down by selling them to me."

Cole never hesitated so much as a breath. "I'll be glad to if you can pay what I did for them. Can you?"

Charlie's pallor disappeared in a hot flush. He knew damn well she couldn't pay what Canfield had. The outrageous prices Rick Slaughter had bid were the crux of the whole miserable situation.

Her chin came up. She had sounded stupid, and it embarrassed her that this man had witnessed it. She hastened to retract her unthinking suggestion. "Of course you can't.

Forget it. It was only an impulse." Any attraction Charlie had felt for Cole Morgan was buried beneath a deep layer of intense resentment. He was a business man, first and foremost, and she best not forget it.

Not that there was anything wrong with Cole or anyone else doing business in a head-on manner. Charlie preferred that approach to beating around the bush. But she felt like a fool in her peach dress and makeup, as though she had anticipated this being a special evening.

Well, she wouldn't make that mistake again. She could be all business, too. Obviously that was to be the tone of their relationship, which was best anyway. A kindly manner while he was stabbing competitors in the back was apparently second nature for Cole Morgan, and his good looks only threw people off guard.

"How do you know I can operate to your satisfaction?" Charlie asked coolly, straightening her shoulders and standing as tall and composed as she could manage.

Cole heaved a relieved breath. For a few minutes there, he'd thought Charlie was going to chuck his offer without giving it a chance. Not that he had to have her operation. He could use it, of course, but he could also get on quite well without it. However, this was the only idea he'd come up with to keep McAllister Lumber Company from going under.

Frankly, Cole wasn't satisfied that he had, even inadvertently, caused the closures of the other local mills. But he wasn't taking the chance with Charlie. She was still operating and he intended to keep her operating, if she would be the least bit cooperative. "I asked around about you," he admitted calmly.

"You asked *my* friends and neighbors about *me*? Wasn't that just a bit presumptuous?"

"They're my friends and neighbors now, too, Charlie, and no, it wasn't presumptuous. I don't go into business deals blindfolded."

"I'm sure you don't," she agreed without a pause, a sharp edge on the words. "So, what did you find out?"

"That you're a good operator. Which, incidentally, I'd already determined myself the day I visited your plant. But I also found out you've got a good reputation in the community. People respect you, professionally and personally."

His spying galled her, but Charlie couldn't say something too blistering when he'd only unearthed good things about her. Well, there was no point in circling the issue. She really had no choice. It was either take the offer or close the mill. And telling fifteen men they were going to be out of a job to salvage her pride made very little sense.

But she would never forget this moment, Charlie vowed, despising Cole Morgan for his self-satisfied role of benefactor. "What are the details of your offer?" she asked, struggling so hard to remain controlled that she felt the pounding of a tension headache in her temples.

Cole reached into his inside coat pocket and came out with a thick fold of papers. "I took the time to stop by my office for this," he explained as he moved close enough to hand her the papers. "It's a projection of operating costs and possible profits based on estimated production."

Accepting the wad, Charlie unfolded it and scanned the columns of neat figures. "I'd like you to look it over thoroughly, when you have the time, of course, and then give me a call." Cole backed off, returning to where he'd left his coffee, and finished it in one swallow. "I think the details are pretty well covered in those figures, Charlie. But if you have any questions, let me know."

Was he going to leave now? Charlie raised her eyes from the pages, wondering how to end this meeting without thanking him. She didn't want to thank him. She'd do almost anything else if she could get out of thanking him. But other than demonstrating out-and-out rudeness, there really wasn't a way to avoid it, was there?

No, she would not be rude. Cole Morgan would never know how much this hurt, not if it killed her to maintain a civil tongue. She would be as businesslike as he was. "Thank you," she said with so much aplomb that she mentally applauded herself. "I'll be in touch as soon as I understand all this," she added, holding the papers up.

"Good enough. Thanks for the coffee, Charlie." Cole started for the door, and when Charlie followed a few steps behind, he stopped to let her catch up. "I'll be expecting to hear from you in a few days," he said with a warm smile.

Charlie ignored it and moved around him to open the front door, knowing there wasn't a smile anywhere in her at the moment. If he wanted smiles, he'd have to look elsewhere. What she felt like doing was bawling like a baby... which she'd probably do the minute he was gone.

"Good night," she offered emotionlessly as she held the door open.

"Good night, Charlie. Talk to you soon." Cole started past, then stopped within inches of her. "By the way, I like that dress." With another smile, he swung on by and crossed the porch, his tall form soon blending with the dark stretch of lawn between house and driveway.

Charlie closed the door quietly, then stood and listened for the sound of his car. A door slammed, the engine started, and in moments there was only the familiar silence of a Montana night.

She didn't burst into tears at all. Nor did she throw something in anger. Oddly, she felt only drained, as though all the intense emotions she'd undergone in Cole's presence had deserted her. She really couldn't even think of all that had happened until she had the downstairs lights off and she was up in her room. Even then she kept her thoughts at bay until she had gulped two aspirin tablets, hung the peach dress back in the closet, washed the makeup off her face and donned a nightgown.

Then, settled in bed, she crooked an arm beneath her head and stared into the dark, finally letting the evening click through her brain. Very little of a personal nature had taken place—that bit of conversation about Cole's background, then his incongruous compliment at the door. Everything else had been business related, and it hit Charlie that Cole was a very strong adversary.

If she had to take his offer—a thought that brought a shudder of repulsion—she would have to be very clear-headed in dealing with him. For one thing, she had to stop thinking of him as "handsome" or as "a nice guy." He was about as nice as a rattlesnake, and certainly as deadly.

The only reason he was making such an offer was obvious. He needed a plant like hers to cut his small logs, and it was much less costly to hire her operation than construct one at the Canfield site. Oh, it was easy to figure out the motive behind Morgan's offer, no doubt the same one that prompted his every move. Money.

"Oh, hell," Charlie muttered, realizing what she'd just come up with. Money was what prompted her moves, too. It was the motivating force behind every business venture in the country, and even in her disgust and frustration with Cole's offer, she found her analysis of the man rather abysmal. Being squeezed into something she didn't like was creating some offbeat thinking, and this was opposed to the clear head she had just decided was imperative.

There had to be a positive side to the situation, Charlie mused, landing immediately on the fact that she wouldn't have to lay her men off. That had been bothering her horribly. She had a good crew, men who gave her a full day's labor for a day's pay, and they looked to her for their livelihood. They certainly deserved consideration in this decision, and for her own appeasement she could look at the arrangement as temporary. Something would break in her favor eventually, and with the mill running she would be ready for it.

Yes, that's how she would view the dismal deal, as a temporary measure, a galling but still fortuitous stepping stone to total independence again. As for Cole Morgan himself, well, she would simply ignore the stirrings of sexual awareness she experienced around him. Complicating an already complicated relationship with furtive thrills and secret palpitations was immature, and a definite waste of time.

A CONFERENCE WITH THE FOREMAN was usual in the morning to coordinate lumber orders with production schedules. This Monday morning, as soon as the conference was over, Charlie headed for her office. Cole's package of computations was on her desk where she'd placed it before the trip down to the plant, and with a cup of fresh coffee, Charlie settled down to study it.

Two hours later she sat back. She had traced the very detailed projection, checking figures with her calculator, and there was no doubt she could make money in the deal. Not a princely sum, but enough to support herself and continue helping Cassie.

Charlie heaved a sigh at the inevitability of her situation. She couldn't turn down the offer no matter how much she'd enjoy telling Cole Morgan to shove it up his nose.

Better yet, how utterly gratifying it would be to throw it in Rick Slaughter's face.

Charlie's skin crawled at the thought of Rick. Cole had said the man was only doing the job he'd been hired to do, supplying Canfield with timber. Well, the theory was understandable. Any plant as large as Canfield needed a full-time employee overseeing its timber department. Yet Rick's overzealousness far surpassed what a normal operation would require. For a fact, Charlie could total up all the timber he'd purchased for Canfield in the past two years and it would be an excessive amount, providing Cole's mill with years and years of future production. Maybe Cole had told him to get out there and buy anything that would make a board, but it seemed to Charlie that the man could have been at least a little sparing of his neighbors.

Besides, even if it didn't make a whole lot of sense, it was much easier to dislike Rick than it was Cole. Charlie sighed again, feeling trapped, and what's more, feeling justified at feeling trapped.

It wouldn't be forever. That was the only comfort she could find in the whole thing.

So she knew she was going to accept Cole's "simple business proposition." But should she appear so eager as to call him this morning with that decision?

"No way," Charlie mumbled, getting to her feet. She kept the company ledgers in a file cabinet and there was always bookwork to be done these days. She really would have to find someone to work in the office as soon as possible, she acknowledged as she pulled out two black-bound ledgers and brought them to her desk.

About half an hour later, deeply involved in entering expenditures in the check register, Charlie jumped a foot when the fire bell rang down at the mill. "Oh, Lord," she whispered, instant terror in her heart. A fire in a sawmill could be nothing more than an electric motor shorting out and causing smoke, or it could be a disaster. There weren't too many things more combustible than sawdust, and although the building was steel and pretty much impervious to flames, there were tens of thousands of dollars of equipment that could be destroyed in the flash of an eye.

Charlie ran all the way to the mill building, dashing inside to see the crew already hosing down flames in the lunchroom. Everyone was trying to help and pure pandemonium was taking place. "Jake, get those men out of the way!" Charlie yelled to the mill foreman.

The men on the hoses were doing a good job, and Charlie pushed through the small crowd to get to their side. So far the fire was contained in one area, within the walls of the crew's lunchroom, and if it could be held there, the only loss would be wooden tables, benches and about fifteen lunch pails.

The area had a volunteer fire department and the mill's fire alarm was wired into a signal siren that sat atop the tallest building in Gibbs. The volunteers were always on the ball, Charlie knew, and should be arriving any minute. It looked, though, as if they wouldn't be needed. Little remained of the fire except smoke and the smell of wet, charred wood.

The men milled around, asking each other how a fire got started in an empty room. Charlie wondered the same thing and discussed it with the foreman. "What do you think happened?" she asked.

Jake, a big, burly man, shook his head. "Beats the heck out of me, Charlie. Some of the men smoke. Maybe one of them left a cigarette burning after their coffee break."

Charlie nodded thoughtfully. There were metal, sandfilled ashtrays in the lunchroom, but it was possible a stray spark had caused the fire.

Just then the volunteers ran in. "What's going on, Charlie?" she heard from several sources.

"It's out," she told them. Unnecessarily, she realized as they stormed the lunchroom. They checked everything over, then Larry Givens, the head of the organization, came back to Charlie.

"Looks like it started under that one table, Charlie."

"From a cigarette?"

"Could be. Well, there's nothing we can do around here now. Let's go," he yelled to his men.

"Thanks, guys," Charlie called as the volunteers filed out of the building. She turned to her crew members. "The lunch pails are ruined. Everyone but the cleanup man and millwright go on home for lunch. Be back in two hours."

As with most sawmill operators, Charlie maintained one man who did nothing but sweep up sawdust and pick up debris around the plant. She also employed a full-time, experienced mechanic to keep the equipment in good order. First she dispatched the cleanup man to do the best he could with the mess in the lunchroom, then she gave her attention to the millwright. "Bob, is there a chance any electrical wiring was damaged in the fire?"

"I'll check it out, Charlie."

Charlie poked around a little longer, then left the nearly silent building and returned to the office. She heard the phone ringing as she got close and sprinted the rest of the way. A trifle winded, she grabbed the phone in the front office. "McAllister Lumber Company."

"Charlie? Cole Morgan. Have you got a fire there? Someone just told me—"

"Already? God, I can't believe the grapevine around here." Charlie collapsed into a chair. "It's out. It was just a small fire in the lunchroom."

"Then everything's okay there?"

Realizing he sounded genuinely concerned, Charlie grew oddly wary. Cole's "nice guy" mask was securely in place, extending even to the tone of his voice. "The damage was limited to the lunchroom," she said quietly.

"Glad to hear it. By the way, I don't suppose you've had a chance to go over that projection yet, have you?"

"I spent some time with it," she admitted.

"And?"

"Well . . . I . . ." She was stammering and knew it. But she didn't want to give in so easily. Why did a near disaster for her work in Morgan's favor? He wouldn't have called without the fire for an excuse.

Cole's resonant voice broke into her thoughts. "Just give me a call when you've made up your mind, Charlie."

She shook her head, unreasonably exasperated at his patience. "Thanks, I'll do that." Charlie put the phone down, giving the instrument a heated glare. She knew darn well she was being petty and that she should have told Cole she intended to accept his offer.

But . . . She would do it tomorrow. Tomorrow was soon enough to relinquish her professional freedom. Besides, she wanted to talk to her sister about it, and she couldn't do that until tonight with Cassie's daytime hours taken up by her new job.

CHARLIE FOUND HERSELF in an awkward position that evening as she tried to explain the situation to Cassie. "It's not the same thing to be cutting someone else's timber," she said for the second time.

"I just don't understand that, Charlie. What difference does it make whose logs you're cutting? The result is the same, isn't it?"

"No, it isn't." Charlie sighed. "It's not the same thing at all. Cole Morgan will be calling the shots, Cass. He'll be telling me what to cut and when to cut it. I'll be filling his orders. I'll lose contact with my buyers. I'll be working for him. Can't you see that?"

"I'm sorry, Charlie, but if the mill is running profitably, I just don't see what the problem is. I know you're an independent woman, but . . ."

"Not anymore," Charlie put in gloomily. "At any rate, I wanted you to know what I'm doing. Frankly, I thought you'd commiserate with me."

Cassie laughed. "I can't feel blue over something that looks like success to me, sis. Actually, it appears that you've managed a rather brilliant solution to what seemed like an unsolvable problem only a short time ago."

"Brilliant! The only brilliance in the arrangement is Cole Morgan's manipulation of a damned rotten situation he caused in the first place. I'm boxed in!"

"Well, as you said, it's only temporary," Cassie soothed.

"Yes, and I won't have to give the crew notice. Those are the only factors keeping me sane."

"Not true, sis. There's one more factor that I know is crucial to your mental health," Cassie teased.

"Which is?"

"Just being able to continue operating that mill. It's something I will never totally comprehend, but I know it's important to you."

Charlie smiled reluctantly. "I guess you're right."

"Oh, by the way, sis, I met an interesting man at the bank."

"Already?" Charlie drawled dryly.

Cassie's laugh rang out. "Yes, already," she mimicked. "His name is Jim Heath and he's terrific-looking and intelligent. He's a loan officer and very impressive. At least I'm impressed with him."

For some reason Charlie thought of Cole. If it weren't for their ghastly business entanglement, she might very well have been saying the same nice things about him. He was definitely terrific-looking, undoubtedly intelligent, and as for impressive, had she ever met a man who had impressed her more? In fact, if she wasn't on the receiving end of what she considered a questionable talent of his in keeping the upper hand, wouldn't Cole Morgan be exactly the kind of strong, bright, sizzlingly attractive man she would give her eyeteeth to get better acquainted with?

It was disgusting, that's what it was, Charlie decided, recognizing a truth she dared not admit too enthusiastically. Cole was dangerous, Cole was ruthless, Cole would do anything to come out number one. And she strongly suspected he didn't only exercise those tendencies in business. A woman who valued her independence better steer clear of a man like him.

Inwardly Charlie cringed a little. Wasn't her imagination getting just a bit carried away? Cole Morgan hadn't exhibited even a tiny personal interest in Charlotte McAllister. All he wanted was the use of her sawmill!

Charlie felt like saying, "Bah, humbug!"

4

COLE RECEIVED CHARLIE'S CALL the next morning. Rick
Slaughter was sitting across the desk; he'd arrived at Cole's
office ten minutes earlier to give him an update on the six
different logging operations Rick supervised for Canfield.
At Cole's unusually pleased expression, a frowning Rick
sank deeper into the chair.

"She's going to take the deal," Cole confided after putting the phone down. He'd mentioned the offer to Rick a
week ago because any phase of Canfield's operation relat-
ing to timber came under the timber supervisor's jurisdic-
tion.

Cole had been supremely gratified to find a man with
Rick's qualifications to head his timber department. Rick
had lived up to his expectations, too, and the dangerously
low supply of standing timber in inventory at Cole's purchase had been increased to a secure level.

Charlie's insinuations that Rick was less than scrupulous
in his methods remained in Cole's mind—a private conjecture he hadn't divulged to the timber supervisor. Cole liked
Rick, he trusted him, and bringing up an apparently un-
founded accusation seemed counterproductive.

Nevertheless, the possibility that Charlie wasn't totally
off the mark was something Cole couldn't entirely dismiss.
He knew he was just a tad more cautious with Rick even
though he suspected the only sin the man might have committed was lording his advantage over the locals, maybe

rubbing them the wrong way. As he'd told Charlie, Rick was only doing the job he'd been hired for.

The one aspect of the whole thing that bothered Cole was that if he'd been a full-time employer in the past two years, he would have been fairer with the timber deals. That Rick had been lacking a certain flexibility didn't make the man anything but a little too loyal to the company he worked for, and Cole was hard-pressed to deem loyalty a crime.

Now, however, after relaying the news that Charlie had agreed to the deal, Cole realized he hadn't expected the supercilious grin he saw on Rick's face, nor his sardonically drawled, "She won't be able to hack it, Cole."

Cole sat back, one eyebrow raised. "Why do you say that?"

"Because she's a woman! Hell, a sawmill's no place for a woman."

"Have you seen her operation?"

Rick squirmed a little, the grin fading. "Well, no, but..."

Cole's eyes narrowed some. "Don't you like Charlotte McAllister, Rick?"

Rick looked away with a cynical laugh. "Hard to like a female who'd rather be a man," he snorted.

That was an impression Cole certainly hadn't gotten from Charlie. Most of the local women wore jeans and boots, from housewives to ranchers, but that didn't make them less female. Sure, Charlie exuded strength and determination; those traits were to be expected in a woman who had chosen the earthy surroundings of the lumber business as a career. But she sure didn't give off any masculine vibes, not to him, anyway.

Slightly resentful of Rick's sarcastic analysis, Cole remarked, "Funny, she never struck me that way."

"Well, she strikes *me* that way," Rick insisted belligerently.

It occurred to Cole that Rick was a little too adamant in his opinion. Was there something personal between him and Charlie? Oddly, the idea of them as a twosome brought some discomfiting sensations, and Cole veered off the subject. "Anyway, the deal's set. I want you to have the loggers start sorting log deliveries to size."

Rick grimaced. "They're not gonna be happy about that. It will take more time in the woods to load out the trucks."

"Not that much more," Cole replied calmly. "I want everything under a twelve-inch diameter sent to McAllister Lumber Company."

"Starting now?"

"Starting as soon as you can talk to the loggers. In the meantime I'll get the attorneys working on the contract. We've also got a lot of small logs in the yard. I'll have those hauled to her plant, too."

"You're going at this in a big way," Rick mumbled sourly.

Cole nodded. "Yes. I think that once Charlie sees the merit of the arrangement, it will be a long-lasting relationship."

IN THE BUSTLE of the next few days Charlie forgot the lunchroom fire. The men had quickly gotten the place back in shape, and between handling the mill, attempting to keep up with the paperwork and looking for a secretary-bookkeeper, Charlie was too busy to worry about something that hadn't done any real damage. She had put up a few more signs cautioning care with cigarettes, but beyond that there was little she could do.

Thursday morning she was stunned when a Canfield truck loaded with logs arrived, and she ran from the office and followed it as it lumbered through the log yard and stopped beside the log scaler's shack. The driver jumped down from the high cab.

"What are you doing here?" Charlie called even before she reached the man.

"Delivering some logs. Weren't you expecting them?"

Jack, the log scaler, ambled up. "What's going on, Charlie?"

"I'm not sure, Jack." Charlie gave the truck driver a sober look. "I don't want you to unload until I talk to Mr. Morgan."

Immediate impatience appeared on the man's face. "I don't have all day."

"It won't take all day. Just wait here a minute." On a dead run Charlie headed back to the office. Truck drivers were notoriously impatient, wanting to make as many trips from woods to mill as they could squeeze in between dawn and sundown. They were paid on the volume of timber they hauled, and Charlie couldn't blame them for not wanting to waste time. But she had to find out what was going on. Cole had mentioned a contract the day she called with her acceptance of the deal, but so far she'd seen no sign of a contract.

She got through to Cole's office without delay, and also got directly to the point. "There's a Canfield truck out here with a load of logs," she said brusquely.

"What's the problem, Charlie?" Cole asked easily.

"The problem is, I wasn't expecting deliveries until we signed a contract."

"Well, as a matter of fact, I have the contract on my desk right now. I planned to bring it over later."

"That's fine, but what about the load that's sitting out here now?"

"Unload it, Charlie. It's only the first one you'll be getting today."

Without a contract? Unloading Cole's logs wasn't a problem from her standpoint, but his making a delivery without something in writing was taking a chance from his side of the ledger. How odd that he was willing to take a risk on her integrity, Charlie pondered. She would have bet anything he never made a business move without tying everything and everyone up legally.

"Have your man scale the logs as usual, Charlie. I'd like a copy of each scale ticket."

"Of course," she murmured, still puzzled by this turn.

"All the steps are listed in the contract. I'll drop it by around three. Is that all right?"

"Three's fine. I'll be here."

On the way back to the log yard Charlie heard another truck arriving, and by two that afternoon, seven loads had been delivered. It was happening. Already. And the seven piles of logs in the yard looked more menacing every time Charlie glanced out the window.

Well . . . in a way they looked wonderful, too. Or, more accurately, they would look wonderful if they were hers.

As it was, Charlie's stomach ached from stress and a sense of events being beyond her control. Was she doing the right thing? Was there anything, anything at all, she could do instead?

The awful truth lay like a lead weight in her midsection. She had committed herself and she was stuck.

Cole strolled into the office at ten to three, larger than life and too good-looking in a white shirt and well-filled jeans. Charlie said a decent "Hello," but couldn't force a smile for the life of her.

"Looks good out there," he said cheerfully with a nod in the general direction of the log yard.

"Yes, well, I guess that's a matter of opinion," Charlie returned stonily.

Cole got right to business. "Here's the contract, Charlie. Read it over and give me a call."

Halfheartedly Charlie accepted the papers. "I'll call you in the morning."

"Don't hurry. There's no rush." Cole smiled as though they were old friends, giving Charlie a flash of white teeth that would glorify a toothpaste ad.

"I'll read it today," she said stubbornly.

Cole shrugged. "Suit yourself."

They were standing in the front office, and Cole looked at the empty desk. "I think you'd better do something about getting some help in here, Charlie."

Her first order? Inwardly Charlie winced. Outwardly she put on a saccharine expression. "I've already been looking," she said sweetly.

"Good." Cole walked around the room, then turned with a snap of his fingers. "Say, I've got a good idea. Let's put my personnel department to work finding the right person for this job."

Charlie stared, hit by a few scathing words she would have liked to unload on him. Her voice was controlled, however, when she replied, "I'd like to find my own secretary, if you don't mind."

"You'd have the final say, Charlie. But I've got a good man in personnel. He could save you a lot of time. Really, I insist. I'll put Roy to work on it this afternoon."

Waves of heat washed through Charlie and crept up to her cheeks. How dare he? The contract wasn't even signed and he was already taking over.

She had to calm herself. She had to or this whole thing would be over before it really began. Nothing looked more desirable than the thought of gleefully ripping up the papers she was holding. Charlie counted to ten.

Cole was at the window again, seemingly oblivious to her agitation. "You've got about two weeks left on your own timber, it looks to me," he observed, scanning the remaining supply of Charlie's own log inventory. "Cut that first and get it out of the way."

He turned. "Do you have very many unfilled lumber orders?"

Charlie's tension only allowed a terse "Some."

"Well, they've got to be taken care of, of course. By the time you need it, I'll have a list of what I want cut brought over."

She could only nod, feeling very much like a resentful child. Other than Cole presuming to hire her secretary, his "orders" weren't out of line. But they grated nonetheless— just as Charlie had known they would. Taking orders just wasn't something she did well, she admitted with renewed fervor, wondering again how she was going to exist within the agreement.

Exist was the key word, Charlie realized. Exist was what she would do, all she could do until she located her own timber supply again. *A temporary arrangement*, she repeated privately, *remember that it's only a temporary arrangement.*

Cole was smiling again. "I guess that does it for now. I'll be waiting for your call on the contract." He walked to the door.

After undergoing so many demoralizing emotions, Charlie remained stock-still. She held the contract and suffered the churning in her middle with a stoic expression, but Cole's departure required some sort of remark, and she could only repeat, "I'll call in the morning."

"Fine." Despite his apparent nonchalance, Cole knew full well why Charlie's striking face looked like the last rose of summer. She didn't like the deal and was only taking it as a last resort. He understood that, but he also felt once they were underway she would see the value of the agreement. She would make good money without the hassle of worrying about a log supply, and he felt certain that once she experienced the more carefree operation, she would feel much better about the whole thing.

From his point of view her apparent distaste would vanish soon enough and was nothing to get alarmed over. In fact, he was already thinking of other things . . . how working together might trigger what was increasingly appealing to him—a more personal relationship. Charlie was the most attractive, interesting woman he'd met in a long time, and he definitely wanted to know her better.

While he stood at the door, ready to leave, he gave her a warm, all-encompassing look, again taking in her unusual beauty, her slender but solid body. Rick was crazier than hell to suggest Charlie wasn't feminine. She wasn't fragile, true, but she sure didn't have any masculine traits. Cole liked strength, in both men and women, and he especially liked Charlotte McAllister. He would like to ask her out, to maybe see her in that peach dress again, to sit across a candlelit dinner table from her and talk about anything *but* business.

But from the guarded look on her face, she'd throw him out of the office if he so much as hinted at a date. The timing was off. Today wasn't a good day for making the initial overture. But someday he'd undo that braid . . . and unbutton that blouse . . . and . . .

"See you, Charlie," he said softly, then he turned and left quickly.

Charlie frowned, puzzled over the oddly personal gleam she'd caught in Cole's blue eyes. He'd been contemplating something, and it sure hadn't been lumber orders!

She gave herself a mental shake, strangely pleased that Cole Morgan might find her attractive and might be working up the nerve to say so. Just let him dare, she thought triumphantly, envisioning the pleasure of putting him in his place. Would anything give her more satisfaction than telling him she didn't mix her personal life with business?

JUST BEFORE CHARLIE LEFT for the day, Pete Dirksen dropped by the office. "Mave wanted me to ask you over for dinner tomorrow night, Charlie. Can you make it?"

"I'd love it, Pete. Thanks. How are things going for you?"

Pete shrugged. "Winding everything up. It's gonna take longer than I thought to close 'er down." He grinned. "Next winter when you're wading through snow and slush, think of Mave and me down in the sunshine."

Charlie laughed. "Oh, I will, believe me, I will. Still planning on Arizona?"

"I think so. We thought about Florida, too, but we both think we'd like a dry climate better." Pete stepped over to the window. "See you got some logs in."

Charlie's heart sank. "I made a deal with Cole Morgan, Pete. I'm going to be cutting his small logs for a while."

"Is that a fact now? Well, that's not so bad, I guess. At least you're still running, Charlie."

"I hate it," Charlie exclaimed passionately. "But it's the only game in town. It's only temporary—that's what I'm hanging on to. I'll get my own timber again."

"Sure you will, honey."

"I keep wondering how Dad would feel about it. What do you think?"

Pete rubbed his whiskery jaw. "Dave would've done anything he needed to keep operating. I wouldn't worry about that too much."

Right behind Pete's departure, Charlie closed and locked the office, made a quick tour of the silent plant—stopping a few minutes to speak to the night watchman—and headed for home. She had the contract with her and planned an evening of reading, not exactly thrilling with what looked to her like too much verbiage to be a simple agreement.

After a shower and a bowl of soup, anticipating one of Mave's delicious dinners tomorrow night, Charlie settled down on the living-room sofa with the contract. It contained all the *wherefore*s and *thereto*s she'd expected, but the gist of the legalese was clear enough and pretty much as she'd understood the arrangement.

Until she got to paragraph fifteen. "The term of said agreement shall be for a period of not less than twenty-four months," it began, saying it again in three different ways, from every conceivable angle, within the same paragraph.

Charlie sat back, stunned. Two years. Cole was tying her up for two years! *No way*, she thought with sudden anger. She had other plans for the future of McAllister Lumber Company, maybe indistinct at present, but plans nonetheless. And they didn't include two years under Cole Morgan's overbearing thumb!

She would clear up paragraph fifteen, first thing in the morning!

CHARLIE WAS SURPRISINGLY CALM when she dialed Canfield's number the next morning. Paragraph fifteen was not a negotiable matter; she would not be tied to two years and she had no problem with telling Cole that.

When she heard his voice she said, "This is Charlie. The contract is unacceptable, Cole. I will not agree to two years."

"May I ask why not?" Cole was sitting in his massive leather chair, and he leaned back comfortably.

"I won't lie about it. I'm looking at this arrangement as temporary."

"I see. Well, I'm sure we can figure something out. Tell you what, I was just getting ready to drive out to the river to take a look at my house. Come with me and we can discuss it."

Charlie bit her lip. Going anywhere with Cole wasn't smart. Despite resolutions to ignore his good looks and a personality she was finding more magnetic every time she saw him, he remained much too attractive in her thoughts. It was easy to conjure up scenes of her telling him to go to hell, but it was another thing to realize she very well might have the opportunity to do so.

Ending their business relationship right here and now didn't set too well either, though. What if he would agree to dropping paragraph fifteen after some discussion of the matter? Already, Charlie realized, she had begun to count on operating steadily throughout a search for her own timber supply. Not having to lay her crew off had been a very important factor in accepting Cole's offer in the first place, and it was still a weighty consideration.

Her personal fears really had to take second place in this, didn't they? Besides, she had probably only imagined the sexy light in Cole's eyes yesterday.

"All right," she finally agreed.

"I'll pick you up in half an hour."

TO HAVE CHARLIE sitting beside him in his pickup was a satisfying sensation, Cole admitted as he drove the river road. The day was sunny and bright, heightening the creamy gold of her hair and revealing, once again, the flawlessness of her complexion. Even without makeup Charlie was a beauty, and she was definitely having an effect on him.

They'd been talking about paragraph fifteen, and Charlie had stated again her stand on the two years. "What length of time would be acceptable?" Cole asked with another admiring glance.

"Does there have to be a time limit on the arrangement?"

"It's not much of a deal without it, Charlie. Look, I think once you've had a chance to work without timber worries, you'll like the deal."

Charlie cocked an eyebrow at him. "You're wrong about that."

"Well, maybe so. Anyway, we should have some kind of time limit in the contract. You tell me what you can live with."

They rode without speaking for a few miles. "Any time limit is all right if we have a thirty day notice clause," Charlie suggested.

"You mean either of us could get out of the contract by notifying the other within thirty days of cancellation?" Cole laughed. "That's pretty loose, Charlie."

Frustration rose within her. He was right, of course. Why have a contract at all if it wasn't binding? But, dammit, she didn't want to be tied down, not without an escape clause. "I'll have to think about it some more," she said grudgingly.

"Think all you want."

"Oh, sure. And in the meantime your trucks are delivering logs. Cole, I'm feeling pretty trapped in this thing," she exclaimed.

"Trapped?" Cole took his eyes from the road again, giving her an amused glance. "I'm not trying to trap you, Charlie. If I wanted to do that, I'd put my efforts to a more satisfying conclusion."

Charlie felt a rush of blood to her face. She might have imagined things yesterday, but there was no mistaking Cole meant something personal now.

Now what was it she had planned to say if he dared cross that line?

Flustered, Charlie turned her head and stared unseeingly out the window. Cole would make their relationship as personal as she would allow, she realized with sudden blinding clarity. And, oh, dear Lord, wasn't that something she would also prefer to their business transactions?

No. Absolutely not. Never! Considering a business arrangement with this man was bad enough; considering anything else was too traitorous to her own sense of ethics to even contemplate. Good grief, it was because of him she was in this ghastly situation!

Why was it getting harder to remember that?

Cole could see what his casual remark had wrought in Charlie. She knew now that he was regarding her as more than just a business associate. But that was all right. He wanted her to know.

In fact, despite his decision yesterday that it was too soon to ask her out, he was glad she knew. Now, when he broached the subject of an evening together, she wouldn't be completely surprised. Yes, he'd bring it up later, on their way back.

He turned off the river road onto his private driveway. It stretched a quarter mile, traversing a rich, green field with a neighbor's grazing horses, and took a sudden, sharp incline to the bluff. "Here we are," he declared as he stopped the truck beside the house.

Lumber and building materials were scattered around, but there wasn't a carpenter in sight. "Shall I wait out here?" Charlie asked.

"Wouldn't you like to see the house? Come on in. It's really great, Charlie. I'd like you to see it."

At least he hadn't expanded the startling subject he'd touched on, Charlie noted gratefully. Still, she got out of the truck with some reluctance. "Where are the carpenters?" she inquired, following Cole to the door.

"I don't know. Maybe off somewhere picking up materials." Cole held the door open for her. "They're almost finished anyway. I should be moving in another week."

The interior of the house was wonderful. Large and airy from high-beamed ceilings and yards of window glass, the place reeked of a delicious "new" smell. The carpets weren't laid yet, and their boots thudded on the bare wood floors. Cole gave her the grand tour, proudly leading her through the empty rooms.

"It's beautiful," she exclaimed several times.

"I plan to move in and then have a decorator put the finishing touches to it," Cole confided. "What do you think about a color scheme? I keep leaning toward blue."

He was asking her opinion? Wouldn't the local gossips get a kick out of that if she spread it around...which she wouldn't, of course. "Blue is lovely. I guess it depends on how masculine you want it to be. As a bachelor, you might want—"

"I don't plan to stay a bachelor forever, Charlie," Cole said teasingly. They were in the kitchen, and he leaned against a gorgeous oak counter and folded his arms. "Some woman will live here eventually. Do you think she'll go for blue?"

Charlie fought the blush she felt staining her cheeks, but embarrassment made her voice sharp. "How would I know what your future wife might like?"

Cole sighed with exaggerated drama. "You're right. Even I can't predict that, can I?"

"Do it in purple," Charlie said peevishly, at which Cole burst out laughing, throwing his head back in genuine amusement.

"Charlie, you're all right," he declared, pushing away from the counter. "Come take a look at the master bedroom. It's really special," he added at the immediate consternation he saw on her face.

The house rang with emptiness, yet Charlie still felt a twinge of nervousness at entering what was obviously going to be Cole's bedroom. It was a huge room with a rock fireplace, an outside balcony, a massive walk-in closet and lots of windows. Cole pushed another door open and Charlie walked into the most incredible bathroom she'd ever seen.

A large whirlpool tub inlaid with blue and white tiles dominated the room. "Looks like you've already decided on blue in here," she commented dryly.

"Yeah. Too bad that tub's not working yet. We could take a whirlpool bath together."

Charlie whirled. "What?"

Cole was in the doorway with his hands high on the frame, a casual pose, but one negated by the smoldering look on his face. "Should I say it again?" he asked softly.

"No . . . I heard you," she stammered.

"I thought you did. It just surprised you, didn't it?"

He looked so big, so overpowering, blocking the door. Battling a suddenly racing pulse, Charlie's eyes darted around the room. "Well," she stated, trying to sound purposeful, "this is very nice, but I think I should be getting back to the mill."

"Already? We just got here. I didn't expect the carpenters to be gone, but Charlie . . ."

How had things changed so quickly? Charlie's eyes grew large and very green. She saw Cole drop his arms from the door frame and step into the room, and she knew he was coming closer for a reason. "Cole . . ." Her voice sounded husky, and even she couldn't tell if his breathily stated name contained a yes or a no.

He stopped within inches. His eyes were a dark, piercing blue, and he put one hand on her arm and slid it slowly up to her shoulder. "I like you, Charlie McAllister," he said softly.

He was still blocking her way to the door. But would she run even if she could? Suddenly lost in the dazing current of electricity passing between them, Charlie couldn't tear her eyes from his. How could she run? She felt his hand move to the back of her neck, and the bonding of his large, warm palm with the sensitive nerve endings there made her knees weak. She actually reeled forward, as though drawn by an irrestible force.

His mouth descended slowly. . .

Charlie closed her eyes, drowning in the exquisite feel of his lips. Warm and firm, they parted, and his tongue circled, asking for entrance. She wasn't thinking, she was only reacting. Her mouth welcomed the hot, moist invader and she felt a surge of desire that threatened to overwhelm her.

Cole gathered her up, drawing her into an embrace that united their bodies from breast to hip. The solidity he'd expected was oddly commingled with a female softness, the unique womanliness of round, full breasts and the firmness of a flat stomach and slender hips. His blood roared in his ears. He'd expected chemistry between them, but this far surpassed anything he could have imagined.

She was kissing him back, raising on tiptoes to clasp her hands behind his head, straining into him, and Cole was getting so aroused that he mentally cursed the fate that had decreed this to happen in a house with a bare, hard floor and not a speck of furniture, let alone a bed. The carpenters could walk in any minute, too . . .

He wanted her, he wanted her to a degree he could hardly believe. And his lips said it with a dizzying kiss and his hands said it in a sensual journey up and down her back and hips.

Charlie was getting the message, loud and clear. Yet she didn't pull away. She felt glued to him, to his hard, muscular chest, to that incredibly arousing maleness in his jeans . . . and his mouth was the sweetest she'd ever kissed, his scent the most desirable she'd ever encountered.

Maybe nothing else could have stopped them, Cole realized when they separated at the sound of men's voices in the house. Charlie looked dazed, and her breasts rose and fell with rapid breaths. Their gazes locked in a heated, knowing exchange. "We'll pick this up later," Cole said gruffly, his eyes promising a thousand delights.

It wasn't until they were driving back that sanity returned to Charlie.

5

PERHAPS IT WAS THE CONTRACT lying on the seat between them, perhaps merely a leveling out of the searing emotions Charlie had just undergone. Whatever the reason, while Cole drove, the reality of what had just happened in the master bathroom of his new house gradually seeped through Charlie's befuddled brain. She hadn't only allowed a kiss . . . she had kissed Cole back with more passion than she had once thought existed on the entire planet!

She knew better now, didn't she?

Where had that consuming, wild, unbelievable response come from?

Charlie drew a very shaky breath, denying herself the luxury of even a peek at Cole, even though she was besieged with a burning curiosity. How was *he* taking this crazy development?

Cole's thoughts were on the past few minutes, too. But he wasn't suffering the remorse Charlie was. In fact, he was busy planning the evening ahead with not a doubt that Charlie was as anxious as he to continue what they had begun. "We'll have dinner tonight," he said quietly.

Conflicting feelings warred for a moment: thankfulness that she had promised dinner with Mave and Pete, regret that she wasn't free.

But where could this go? She couldn't do business with Cole and hold hands with him on the side. Muddying an already cloudy relationship with romance wasn't sensible, and it wasn't a matter of choosing which relationship she would rather have. She had to do business with him; she didn't have to get personally involved.

"I already have plans for this evening."

Startled, Cole gave her a quick look. "You do?"

Charlie nodded and looked away, chewing her bottom lip with uncertainty.

"Tomorrow's Saturday," Cole pressed. "Are you busy tomorrow?"

Oh, Lord, what should she do? She shouldn't even like this man. She had to work for him. She had to take his orders, run her business at his whim. And there was still the contract to iron out. What about that damned time limit?

Facing him uneasily, Charlie realized the answer she'd planned, should anything like this happen—the one about not mixing her personal life with business—tasted like bitter bile in her mouth. "Let's not complicate our relationship by seeing each other socially," she managed aloud.

Dismay struck Cole. "Seeing each other socially has nothing to do with our business relationship!"

Was he serious? An examination of his taut features said he was. Very. Charlie shook her head. "I'm sorry. I don't see it that way. I can't work for you during the day and see you at night."

"You mean it's a question of one or the other?"

Confused, Charlie fell silent. What did she mean? Even she didn't clearly know. How could she pass something so nebulous on? There were layers of complications, old events, new events, doubt, mistrust. There was no easy way to bypass all of that and pretend it wasn't a painfully abiding part of herself.

She tried. Cautiously. "We have this—" Charlie picked up the contract "—to sort out." Her tone indicated her priorities.

"If you're referring to that thirty-day clause you mentioned, you've got it." Cole gave her a hard look, not believing she was taking this attitude. "See how easy it is to eliminate dissension?"

Charlie's eyes widened. He did that because of that wild scene in the bathroom! On the drive to his house, she'd been sure the time clause was going to be a major problem, and now, in the blink of an eye, he'd reduced it to nothing.

It hit Charlie wrong. How dare he make a business concession based on a few minutes of intimacy? She didn't want favors because he found her sexually exciting.

Charlie felt a mushrooming resentment. It wasn't her fault they were in this unnerving state of confusion—it was his! And it had its roots well planted in the fertile ground of the past two years of worry and sleepless nights. How many hours had she spent walking the floor, or dashing about the countryside like a madwoman looking for private timber?

And he expected her to just forget all that?

Well, she would if she could. She didn't like dwelling unhappily on the irrevocable past. And maybe if things were different today, if she were operating the mill under normal circumstances, the past wouldn't be so meaningful. But it was still going on. And it would go on as long as she was tied to Canfield.

No, there was no chance of anything personal between her and Cole Morgan. Their futures might be connected, but only through this contract.

They were nearly at the mill, and from the look on Cole's face he wasn't through yet. Charlie steeled herself for a barrage of arguments as the pickup turned onto her property and stopped.

Cole switched the key off and turned in the seat. "I intend seeing you outside of our business arrangement," he said, determination radiating from the depths of his blue eyes.

She shook her head. "No."

"Yes."

"Cole, I don't want to argue about this. I have work to do." Charlie reached for the door handle, but a hard hand on her arm stopped her flight. "Please!" she protested sharply.

Cole spoke softly, belying the urgency he felt and the strength of the fingers around her arm. "You felt exactly what I did at the house and you're trying to deny it. Let yourself like me, Charlie. Don't put a wall up between us."

Her breath caught. "That wall was erected months ago, and it wasn't my doing."

"Maybe not, but you're hiding behind it all the same. Give us a chance. I have a feeling we could have something very special."

Charlie swallowed hard. How influencing he was. It would be so easy to say yes to everything he asked, or even hinted at with aura and the warmth of a pleading expression. If things were different . . . if she had met Cole under different circumstances . . . if . . .

"No," she said huskily. "I can't get involved with you."

"Maybe you already are."

"Not yet," she denied, wondering if she was lying, if maybe he was right and she was already too emotionally entangled to just forget what had happened.

Whatever, she had to try. The only really important thing between them was this contract. And she couldn't live up to it and carry on with Cole at the same time. It simply wasn't in her to do both.

Cole studied her obstinate expression with an urge to shake some sense into her. "This is ridiculous, Charlie," he muttered in a slightly angry tone.

"I have to go." She tugged against his grasp.

He held on for another few moments, then released her arm abruptly. "I'll have a new contract drawn up with the change you want," he said coolly. "I'll bring it by as soon as it's completed."

"Thank you." Charlie opened the door and slid from the seat. "Goodbye," she mumbled, walking away immediately. It didn't calm her nerves to feel Cole's eyes on her every step of the way.

The truck didn't start until she was inside and wishing with every cell in her body that she hadn't gone with him today.

MAVE DIRKSEN WAS a wonderful cook. She could do more with a ham and scalloped potatoes than anyone else Charlie knew. Not usually a big eater, Charlie did justice to the meal and was already uncomfortable when Mave offered peach cobbler for dessert.

"Not for me, Mave, thanks. If I ate one more bit I'd burst."

Pete and Mave had some, though, and Charlie enjoyed a second cup of coffee while they indulged. Dinner conversation had consisted mainly of the Dirksen's future plans, but it was Mave who had a final remark on the subject. "I'm just not sure about selling this house yet, Charlie. I think we'll buy one of those little trailers and head south this fall with it. Uprooting ourselves without a trial just isn't sensible."

Charlie nodded at the tiny, birdlike woman. Mave was the talker in the Dirksen family, and Charlie knew from years of friendship that Pete usually listened to her. There was a very real love between Pete and his gray-haired wife, and Charlie had always enjoyed being around the two of them. With her own mother gone so long and little memory of her parents' relationship, Charlie had always admired the affectionate give-and-take between the Dirksens.

Sitting at their table, pondering their plans, Charlie could only agree with Mave's common-sense assessment. But after saying so, she couldn't help adding with a touch of bitterness, "You two wouldn't be leaving at all if your mill wasn't out of timber."

Pete shoved his empty dessert bowl away and sat back. "Well now, I'm not so sure about that, Charlie. It's time to quit." His eyes twinkled. "Maybe I should say retire, huh? Sounds a lot fancier."

"Rick Slaughter thought so, didn't he?" Charlie commented dryly.

"Yeah. Well, I don't pay too much attention to Rick's snide remarks," Pete laughed. "And Mave sure doesn't, do you, honey?"

Mave snorted. "That Rick. He's one of a kind, all right." The little woman's eyes went to Charlie. "What about that fire you had at the mill, Charlie?"

"Did you hear about it?"

"Heck, yes. Everyone in the county has by now. What happened?"

Charlie shook her head. "We think it was a careless smoker. Actually the damage was minimal and I didn't even turn it into the insurance company. But it sure scared me for a few minutes."

"I can well imagine," Mave agreed vehemently. "Pete, did you tell Charlie about Mr. Morgan stopping by?"

"What?" Charlie sat up straighter. "Did Cole Morgan visit you, Pete?"

Pete grinned. "Sure did. Surprised the heck out of me."

"What did he want?"

"Well, you know, I have a feeling he was going to offer me the same deal he gave you."

"You're not serious!" Charlie knew her mouth must be hanging open a foot.

"He never did get around to it," Pete cautioned. "But I think it was because I told him about me and Mave's plans. Heck, Charlie, Morgan's a pretty nice fellow."

Charlie slumped in her chair, feeling deserted all of a sudden. She and Pete had always been single-minded in their opinion of Canfield and Rick Slaughter, and to her, that included Mr. High and Mighty Morgan, too. Now Cole had turned on the charm and succeeded in altering Pete's outlook, and it didn't feel good to be the only one on her team.

"He's a good-looking devil," Mave laughed. "Just his name sends the young women around here into a tizzy. I was talking to May Hale the other day and . . ." Mave went into some of the local gossip and Charlie listened to what appeared to be news of a quickly developing admiration society for the too, too wonderful Mr. Morgan.

It galled her, but all Charlie could do was pretend interest in the local belles' opinion that Cole Morgan was the catch of the century until Mave ran down. Then her natural spirit and opposing viewpoint leaped to life. "Everyone seems to be forgetting the damage the man has done in this community," she declared passionately. "Two years ago there were . . . how many operating mills, Pete?"

Pete stirred, a frown appearing on his leathery face. "Now, Charlie, you have to be fair about that. Lester Mann wouldn't have made it with an entire national forest behind him. He was a lousy businessman and we both know it. Some of those other mills were shoestring operations without a chance, too."

Deflated, Charlie stared at her old friend. "Pete, nothing will ever change my opinion about Morgan's culpability.

Canfield aced every other bidder out of the picture with outrageous bids. You know that."

A sigh lifted Pete's bony shoulders. "I know. But, honey, a small operation just can't compete with a big one on cost efficiency. Morgan cuts so much more lumber for less than it costs you or me per thousand board feet, he can pay more for timber."

"That doesn't make it right," Charlie returned sharply.

"No, but it's what a small operator is facing, Charlie."

Charlie chewed her lip thoughtfully. "Do you think small businesses have no chance anymore, Pete?"

Pete tugged on an ear, giving it some thought, and Mave took advantage of the pause to put in, "Small business is the backbone of America, Charlie. If Pete were your age he'd be right in the middle of the fracas and we all know it. Pete, stop discouraging the girl!"

Pete grinned guiltily. "Yeah, you're right. I'm tired, Charlie, old and tired. Don't pay what I said any mind. You're a darned good operator and if I was your age, like Mave says, I wouldn't be quitting either."

Charlie left the Dirksens later with a lot to think about. She despised Rick Slaughter and that sentiment needed no thought. But what about Cole? It wasn't possible to despise him no matter how hard she tried, she knew, because she'd been attempting that very emotion ever since he'd brought her back to her office, and she hadn't even partially succeeded.

But was it possible she was judging him a little too harshly in the timber matter? Was there such a vast disparity in methods of operation between a large and small sawmill that Cole hadn't done anything other than what he'd had to?

Damn! She was getting glimpses of his side of the issue and she didn't want to. Little by little her defenses were crumbling, and if she ever reached the point of not having any, where would that leave her? Blithely operating her plant under Canfield's heavy shadow?

Charlie's ingrained independence recoiled at the thought. Damned if she'd allow herself to get to that point! The whole community might be gradually warming to Cole Morgan, but that didn't mean she had to join them.

And as far as that episode in his house went, she would definitely make sure it never happened again!

CASSIE CALLED ON SUNDAY during her lunch break at the bookstore. "Just wanted to say hi," she exclaimed, "and find out how you're getting along."

"All right, I guess," Charlie replied desultorily.

"Did you take Mr. Morgan's offer?"

Charlie admitted she had and went into details of the contract and paragraph fifteen. "Anyway, we got that resolved," she finished lamely, disturbed again over how the resolution had developed. It still made her uncomfortable to think Cole's concession might have been prompted by emotion, and she wondered now if he was sorry about it.

Cassie was more interested in another subject, however, Charlie realized when her sister brought up Jim Heath again. "We had dinner together last night," Cassie confided.

"You're obviously still impressed," Charlie teased.

"More than ever."

Charlie sighed, a touch envious at her sister's unrestricted feelings. Deep down she knew Cole Morgan moved her like no other man ever had, but there were so many restrictions on her feelings she dared not even acknowledge them. But that wasn't Cassie's fault.

"I'm glad you met a man you really like," Charlie said sincerely.

"Thanks, sis. By the way, are you planning the normal Fourth of July this year?"

The holiday was traditionally McAllister Lumber Company's annual picnic date, and with Charlie so caught up in more basic concerns, the picnic hadn't entered her mind. Now she groaned. "Cass, I hadn't even thought of it. I'll have to get working on it."

"I'll have time off, sis, and I was thinking of asking Jim to attend. Would you mind?"

"Not only wouldn't I mind, I'd be thrilled to meet him."

"Great. I'll do my best to arrange it. Well, I better get back to work. Talk to you later, sis."

Charlie put the phone down with a sigh. Where would she find the time to work on picnic plans?

CANFIELD LOGGING TRUCKS began rolling in early Monday morning and continued throughout the day. The little mill was a beehive of activity, the way it used to be, and Charlie sensed high spirits among the crew. It was obvious they didn't care whose logs they'd be cutting as long as their jobs were secure again, and Charlie could see just how worried they must have been. That was the one aspect of the whole miserable deal that made her feel good—job security for her men.

That morning, too, Charlie interviewed two applicants for the office position but was disappointed to find neither of them qualified for the very diversified job. She had to have someone with bookkeeping and secretarial skills, and she'd known ahead of time not many people excelled at both.

She was at her desk trying to wade through the ever-increasing piles of paperwork when she heard someone come in, and her pulse picked up when she recognized Cole's bootsteps. He had a heavy, positive walk. There was no mistaking his purposeful stride. Charlie's every sense jumped to full alert, and she rose slowly in anticipation of his appearance in the doorway, wondering if the contract had been corrected so quickly.

"Hello, Charlie," Cole said quietly.

"Hello," she echoed, aware of a slicing awareness shooting through her from head to toe. Would his incredible looks ever cease to be a shock to her system? she wondered behind the more pertinent question of why he was there.

"I'd like to talk to you," Cole announced. "Have you got a few minutes?" He scanned her cluttered desk. "Roy's interviewing job applicants today."

"I interviewed two people, too," she said dispassionately, strangely unable to muster up any emotion on the subject of who found her secretary. They'd already gone around on that topic, and in the long run, what did it matter? She had to have help, one point they saw eye to eye on.

Charlie gestured to the two chairs in front of her desk. "Would you like to sit down?"

"Thanks." When Cole had sat, he unabashedly stared across the desk, taking his time in absorbing the golden glint of her hair, a mouth he remembered too well as soft and ardent, slender arms encased in blue chambray and a figure that gave him a jolt every time he saw Charlie.

He had decided over the weekend, two days that had been oddly lonely, that he couldn't ignore what had happened at his house and he couldn't let Charlie ignore it, either. There were kisses and there were kisses, some important, some with no more emotion than a handshake. What had passed between him and Charlotte McAllister was in a class by itself, not easy to define, but recognizable as unique all the same. He wasn't about to let it drift out of his life like a puff of smoke.

"I think we should clear the air." Cole leaned forward in the chair, sitting, Charlie realized in a burst of understanding, much like a panther ready to pounce. He was here to press her into something!

She become immediately wary and put on a guarded expression to conceal her confusing thoughts. Was there a speck of glee somewhere in all the smothering denial in her head that he hadn't given up? Maybe. Obviously the spark he'd ignited in his house on Friday wasn't entirely extinguished, but she'd be damned if it was going to influence her. "I don't want an argument, Cole, so if that's what you came for..."

"A discussion, Charlie. Just a discussion."

Her eyes darted fitfully. She could ask him to leave or simply refuse to discuss anything personal. Options vied for prominence, resulting in a discouraged sigh, and although she knew perfectly well what he'd meant, she asked, "Discuss what?"

"You and me."

Charlie knew her color was changing. Cole's direct approach was unnerving. "I think we covered that well enough the other day."

"We didn't cover it at all. You wouldn't discuss it then, either. Charlie, what's the problem here? I know you're not happy about running your mill for me, but dammit, it's a good deal. I think deep down you know it, too."

On several other occasions in Cole's presence Charlie had felt anger, hot, scorching anger that she'd suppressed to maintain the uneasy peace she knew existed between them. True, there were also moments, such as Friday night after dining with Pete and Mave, that she wondered about her accusing attitude where Cole was concerned. But his continual lack of regard for what she might be going through over his "good deal" was getting on her nerves.

Maybe she'd been remiss in not speaking to Rick a long time ago about the dire timber situation in the area. Maybe she had even misjudged Cole's motives when he'd been away so much of the time and possibly not privy to the actual machinations of his timber supervisor. But right now, to have him sitting across her desk and stating in so many words that she should be grateful instead of resentful was too much.

If Pete or Mave or any number of other longtime friends had been in the office, they would have seen the danger signs of Charlie's developing fury. Her eyes flashed with green sparks, her mouth became grim and her skin had paled a few shades. She spoke tensely, and her tone implied, *You're asking for this, Cole Morgan.*

"All right. Let's get it clear once and for all. I will not—let me repeat that—I will not get involved with you. My reasons are very basic. One, I don't completely trust you. Two—"

Cole stopped her with a harsh "Why don't you trust me?"

Charlie's anger was getting stronger. "Because I find it hard to trust anyone who doesn't give two hoots about other people. You're for Cole Morgan, no one else."

"That's a crock. Why would I make that deal with you if I didn't care about other people?"

"Oh, come on. I wasn't born yesterday, Cole. You need my operation. We both know it."

He scoffed right in her face. "I don't need your operation. I can put my own small-log mill in. I told you that."

"But it would be very costly to do."

"Cost isn't the problem you think it is. Mistrust isn't fair, Charlie. You don't have one solid reason for mistrusting me."

That was the final straw. Charlie rose to her full height, which wasn't very impressive when Cole got up, too, and towered over the desk and her and everything else in the room. But she was so livid she didn't even notice. "When my father got ill and I took over this plant, we also owned a section of timberland. We still own the land, but instead of forest, it's nothing but small trees and brush now. Would you like to know why? It's because of you, because in the past two years I haven't been able to outbid your precious timber buyer and I had to log that land to keep operating."

Charlie paused only long enough to catch her breath. "Rick does you a good job. I hope you know *how* good. He told me he was only doing that job, and you reinforced his weaseling out of any wrongdoing by saying he was only doing the job you hired him for. Well, there were once a half-dozen mills operating in this area and now there are two, yours and mine. Does that please you? Does it give you a sense of satisfaction to know you've nearly rid western Montana of any competition?"

Cole was staring at her as if she were demented, and the look made Charlie angrier still. "If you want to cancel the agreement, go right ahead. I'm just about fed up with this whole thing anyway. Pick up your damned logs and leave me alone!"

"Lady, you're so far out of line, I'm tempted! But a deal's a deal." Cole swirled and in a single long stride was at the door. "Don't worry about me bothering you again. I won't. When the contract is ready, I'll have it delivered."

It took Charlie a full two minutes of staring at the vacant doorway to calm down before she realized Cole was really gone. Her legs suddenly buckled and she fell back into her chair, weak with the aftermath of the storm that had gripped her.

Well, she'd finally let him have it. Did she feel better?

She wasn't much of a weeper, but the urge to just let go was overwhelming and she put her face in her hands and let the tears flow. Dammit, she shouldn't be crying. She should be relieved that the bottled-up feelings she'd been enduring had finally been said.

He'd deserved every word, too, every hotly flung word.

Then why did she feel like something important had just died?

He shouldn't have come, he shouldn't have pressured her. She'd been doing admirably at keeping her anger under control. If only he hadn't pressured her.

WHEN COLE ARRIVED back at Canfield, he strode through the office looking as dark and tense as a thundercloud. He stopped at his secretary's desk and said, "Find Rick Slaughter and tell him I want him in my office right away."

Then he proceeded into his inner sanctum, closed the door and paced. It was ten minutes before Rick rapped once and sauntered in. "You wanted to see me, Cole?"

"Yes. Close the door."

"Sure." Once he'd complied, Rick stood by uncertainly.

"Sit down," Cole said gruffly. He hadn't wanted to confront Rick on this, but Charlie's continuing accusations had to be laid to rest. "Were you aware that the small mills in the area were without timber and closing down because of it?"

Rick gave a sneering laugh. "Who told you that? Charlie?"

"It doesn't matter who told me. Is it true?"

"Cole, I never did one thing that wasn't part of my job. You hired me to buy timber. I bought timber. It's not my fault, and sure as hell not yours, if the competition couldn't stand the heat. Hell, there wasn't a good operator in the bunch."

"That's an attitude I will not tolerate, Rick. I've owned mills in four other states and I never ran anyone out of business before."

"Charlie's just a whiner. Don't listen to her."

Cole tensed. "I know you two have a problem, but Charlie is not just a whiner. Dammit, Rick, if you knew what was going on, why didn't you tell me?"

"Cole, believe me, I'm pretty damned busy with all I've got to do. I spend more than half the week out in the woods with the loggers and the rest of it on paperwork. How would I know what's going on at the other mills?"

"That will be a whole lot easier to do now that there'll only be one, other than Canfield," Cole declared sarcastically.

"Well, that's not my fault," Rick repeated sullenly.

Cole took an exasperated breath. "All right, forget it. I just wish you would have kept me better informed."

Sensing dismissal, Rick got up slowly. "I don't appreciate that woman making trouble for me," he muttered.

"That woman happens to be important to me," Cole replied coldly, surprising himself not only by stating such a thing as fact, but because it was true.

And after Rick left, Cole admitted it again, cursing under his breath as he did so. Falling for a woman who made it plain she wanted no part of him was probably the dumbest thing he'd ever done.

6

ON WEDNESDAY Charlie had two contacts with Canfield people, neither of whom was Cole. Roy Waverly, Canfield's personnel manager, called to say he was sending a young woman over the next morning who he felt sure was exactly what Charlie was looking for. Later in the day the contract was delivered by another Canfield employee.

Charlie asked the man to wait, read it over quickly—noting the thirty-day clause—signed it and told him to bring it back to Mr. Morgan. With a "that's that" sigh she returned to her desk, only to glare at the books and numbers in front of her. She simply could not deal with one more number today, and she put everything away and turned to a more pleasant task, planning the company picnic.

That afternoon she posted a sign on the bulletin board in the men's lunchroom, an announcement that the picnic would be held in the Gibbs city park on the Fourth of July as usual, and went home early.

Charlie had been unsettled ever since the harsh words with Cole, and one thing stood out in her mind: she was deeply, unhappily sorry she had lost her temper. Even defending her anger with righteously indignant memories of the past two years didn't alleviate the gnawing remorse, and the terrible scene was keeping her emotionally agitated.

She arrived home with the hope that a leisurely bath and a little peace and quiet would still her restless heart. As it turned out, the long evening alone was worse than if she'd grubbed through another three or four hours of book work, and she went to bed wishing she could undo Monday's altercation.

Should she call and apologize?

Charlie thought about it and realized something very basic. She wasn't sorry she had finally told Cole how she really felt. She was only sorry she had said it in anger.

Temper was a costly emotion, she admitted sadly, really only demeaning the person who indulged in it. The target of a furious outburst usually came out as a victim, while the one doing the shouting looked like a fool. Was that how Cole viewed her now—as a fool?

Oh, that hurt. That possibility hurt so much Charlie didn't linger on it. She wanted Cole Morgan's respect, even if that was the most intimate feeling she dared allow. His silence since Monday evidenced his intention of doing as he'd said, to "leave her alone," and while she could deal with that, she hated the thought of him ignoring her with such a negative opinion.

Gloomily Charlie stared into the dark until she finally dropped off to sleep. Her next conscious thought was an irritable *Who's calling in the middle of the night?* as she reached for the bedside phone. "Hello," she groaned.

It was Leon Ames, her night watchman, and he was speaking so fast she could hardly grasp the words. "There's a fire!" was the gist of the brief conversation, though, and Charlie slammed the phone down and leaped out of bed, all signs of drowsiness buried in the terror of one word: fire!

She pulled on jeans, a sweatshirt and boots in quick succession, grabbed up her shoulder bag and raced from house to pickup. The three-mile drive was accomplished in as many minutes, and the first sight of a red glare in the black night made her ill.

Frantically Charlie turned off the highway and drove the truck as close to the mill building as she could get it. The volunteers were already there, stringing hoses, shouting, finding all the drama in this fire that had been missing in the small lunchroom blaze.

It was in the lumber piles, Charlie realized, torn between gratitude that the building wasn't on fire and horror that thousands of dollars of shipment-ready lumber was literally going up in smoke.

The leaping flames reflected on men's faces, men who were running, men who, though volunteers in a rural fire department, knew what they were doing. Every year Charlie made a substantial donation to the Three Forks Volunteers, and she thanked God for them now. In the dazing activity, with the crackle of flames burning stacks of dry boards, Charlie spotted the night watchman. "Leon!" she yelled, picking her way through men and hoses to reach him.

Leon rushed toward her. "Charlie! Damn, I don't know what happened! I was having my lunch and I smelled smoke and—"

"It's not in the mill, is it?"

"Not yet. These boys are good, Charlie. I think they'll stop it from spreading."

The noise was unique to such a horrifying scene. Shouts, curses, the whoosh of water as the hoses let loose a high-pressure deluge, the hiss and sizzle of dying flames as the water smothered them.

It was only about fifteen minutes before it was out, but it was a long fifteen minutes to Charlie. She had leaned against the side of the pickup and watched her hard-earned lumber turn to wet charcoal.

The lights of a vehicle coming up behind her prompted a turn of her head, and dully she registered Cole jumping out of his truck and making tracks in her direction. "How bad is it?" he called even before reaching her, intense concern on his face.

"Bad enough. They're mopping up now. It was in the lumber stacks. I doubt if much can be salvaged," Charlie said wearily.

Larry Givens, the volunteers' chief, walked up. "It's pretty much out, Charlie. We'll hang around for a while and make sure there aren't any stray sparks."

Charlie pushed away from the support of the pickup. "Thanks, Larry. I'm going up to the office and make some coffee. I'd like to talk to you before you leave, all right?"

"Sure, Charlie."

"Want some coffee?" Charlie said to Cole without enthusiasm. She felt limp and lifeless, too drained to even feel anger at this cruel twist of fate.

"I'll come with you," Cole replied, noncommital about the coffee.

Physically as well as mentally bogged down, Charlie climbed into her truck and drove to the office, aware, without really caring one way or the other, that Cole's pickup was right behind her. She was dazed, she knew, hardly able to think, and Cole's presence made as much sense as anything else. Inside the little office, with Cole standing by silently, she prepared the coffeepot and switched it on.

"What happened?" Cole asked softly, aware of Charlie's abnormal vibes. He was getting confusion from her, shocky tension, as though she were strung out and stretched too thinly.

But there was something else different about her, too. Her hair was down, hanging thick and glorious around her shoulders, and he couldn't get enough of seeing her this way. She must have been in bed. She must take the braid out at night. The thoughts mingled with the concern Cole was feeling.

Her gaze swept his way, her eyes pale with a fatigue that had nothing to do with sleeplessness. "Leon—he's the night watchman—Leon said he was on his lunch break and smelled smoke. That's all I know."

Cole rubbed his jaw. "Funny place for a fire to start."

The comment sank in, slowly at first, then with meaning. "Yes, it is, isn't it? There's nothing electrical, no equipment, nothing out there except lumber." Out of the blue it came to Charlie that her hair must be flying every which way because Cole was giving it an inordinate amount of attention. Self-consciously she smoothed it down, stifling an urge to apologize for her appearance. In an emergency people didn't stop to fix their hair, and this certainly had been an emergency. No, she might owe Cole an apology, but it wasn't because she looked a fright.

Normal feelings were returning and Charlie suffered some of the worries she'd gone to bed with. This might be a good time to bring up Monday. Was it? Did she have the strength or the will to insinuate a personal note into this terrible night? What had brought Cole along anyway? Of course, he might have heard the fire siren in town—which she had obviously slept through—or he could have just been passing by.

Whatever, it had been nice of him to stop. Maybe he wasn't as disgusted with her as she'd been fearing.

Lord, her legs felt mushy. Charlie teetered to the desk and sat on a corner of it. She felt a tremor building in her body, a reaction to too much tension.

Cole moved closer. "Are you all right?"

"Just a little shaky."

"I'll get you some water. Stay there," he flung over his shoulder as he hastened to the bathroom. He was back in seconds with a paper cup of water. "Drink it," he commanded.

"Thank you." With a trembling hand Charlie brought the cup to her lips. She drank it all and took a deep breath. "Thanks," she repeated. Cole was standing very near, watching her closely.

"Feeling better?" he asked anxiously.

"Yes, thanks. Cole, how would a fire get started out there?"

"I don't know. Let's see what Larry thinks. While we're waiting for him, why don't you sit on something more comfortable?" Gently he took her arms and brought her to her feet. "Come on, walk around the desk and use the chair."

No one had ever babied Charlie or spoke to her in a mothering tone of voice. She was always the strong one, the person other people looked to for comfort. It was strangely pleasing to have Cole's hands on her and his wonderful blue eyes relaying concern.

"You're trembling." Cole stared down at her. The ceiling light had turned her hair to pure gold and she looked like she needed a friend so badly he ached for her. "Charlie . . . damn . . ." he said huskily, drawing her forward. His arms settled around her and he released a shaky breath when her head rested on his chest.

Charlie felt tears in her eyes. She was only getting emotional because of the fire, she thought dimly, too secure up against the hard strength Cole emitted to back away and deny she needed him at this moment. She needed something, someone, and Cole was here, and offering solace.

"Cole...I..." Her voice cracked, she felt choked, and the tears turned to full-fledged sobs.

Cole stroked her hair, feeling its silky texture with the satisfaction of knowing he'd predicted it would feel like this. "Cry it out," he murmured, pressing his lips to the scented strands.

"God, I feel so...beaten," she rasped unevenly as the sobs finally diminished.

"You've had a rough time of it, sweetheart. Things will get better. I promise."

The endearment sank in. *Sweetheart?* Charlie's heart did a flip, and she was suddenly aware of how he was holding her. Jeans-clad thighs rode against hers, her tears were staining his shirt, his hands were in her hair, touching, caressing. Where she'd been almost chilled, a seeping warmth was beginning. She was still trembling, but now it was from a subtly different cause. Where the embrace had been kindly and comforting, now it was becoming sensual.

Charlie cleared her throat. "I need to find a tissue," she whispered huskily. Without looking at him she escaped his arms and went into the bathroom. Her mirrored reflection startled her. Her eyes were wet, her hair wild, her nose pink. She should look terrible, but she didn't. There was an underlying excitement in her expression, and it was because of Cole.

It didn't matter, did it? It didn't matter how often she told herself they couldn't have a personal relationship, she liked him. She liked him a lot. Much, much more than she should.

The moment was poignant, the admission painful, and Charlie tried to shake it. She couldn't. It stayed with her while she dampened a paper towel and wiped her eyes. She had deeply rooted feelings for Cole, and they weren't something she could brush aside any longer.

Now what? What was the next step in their very strange association? There was the contract and her unwanted subordination within it; there were old suspicions and accusations that still roamed restlessly in her soul; there was the man, Cole Morgan, who stood so tall and overwhelmingly influencing....

Charlie's emotional meandering was interrupted by what she could hear from beyond the bathroom. Larry Givens had come in and he and Cole were talking. Quickly Charlie smoothed her hair back, squared her shoulders and opened the door.

The men were examining a twisted, charred chunk of something yellow. Charlie walked over. "What is it?" she asked.

Larry responded. "A gas can, one of those plastic gas cans."

Charlie drew a sharp breath. "Where did you find it?"

"In the lumberyard. Could it belong to the mill?"

"Well..." Now that she knew what it had been before the heat of the fire had deformed it, Charlie could see it was a very common article, and yes, it was likely several of these were in the tool room right now. They were also a familiar sight on the back of dozens of pickups in the area. Along with tools, people in these parts carried gas cans—loggers especially, since they had chain saws to keep fueled for their work.

Charlie sighed. "It could belong to the mill, or a hundred other people."

"That's what Cole and I were just talking about," Larry agreed gruffly. "There's no way of telling who dropped it out there, but, Charlie, I think the fire was deliberately set."

She had already suspected that, Charlie realized, but still, hearing it from a man who understood fires was a blow. Digesting the dismal news, Charlie looked to the door as Leon walked in. Immediately she told him Larry's information.

Leon nodded through the brief tale. "That's what I thought, too," he said. "I made rounds just before I went to the lunchroom and there sure wasn't a fire then."

"Did you hear anything out of the ordinary?" Larry inquired.

Leon shook his head. "Nothing, Larry, sorry."

"Well, I'm gonna have to notify the sheriff, Charlie. He'll probably be around tomorrow."

"I understand." Charlie met Cole's troubled gaze. They both knew arson wasn't covered under ordinary fire insurance. But sometimes it could be construed as vandalism, which was covered, a complexity of interpretation to be ironed out with the insurance company. The lunchroom fire would complicate things, too, as she hadn't filed a claim. "I still think the first fire was an accident," Charlie said thoughtfully.

"Could be it gave someone ideas," Larry mused. "Well, I'll be going now. Talk to you tomorrow, Charlie. Night, Cole, Leon."

Leon left soon after and Charlie went over to the full pot of coffee and switched it off. "Who would do this, Charlie?" Cole asked, watching her almost warily, worrying about her and why someone would purposely put a torch to her property.

She shook her head grimly. "I haven't the foggiest idea. I can't even imagine someone hating me enough to want to destroy the mill." Charlie dug out her key ring. "I'm going to lock up and go home, Cole. Thank you for stopping."

"No problem," Cole murmured. "You look tired, Charlie," he told her as they left the office and Charlie turned the lock.

"Maybe I'm more discouraged than tired." She sighed.

"That's understandable right now, but it could have been kids. Maybe the fire was a sort of stupid, irrational prank."

Charlie didn't have the strength for conjecture and only murmured a dull "Maybe." They had reached her truck. "Good night, Cole. Thanks again."

She drove home with Cole's headlights reflected in the rearview mirror. When she turned into her driveway, he tooted his horn once and drove on past, and it was apparent he'd been making sure she got home okay.

AT A QUARTER OF EIGHT the next morning a young woman strolled into the office. "Miss McAllister? I'm Joan Summers. Mr. Waverly sent me over."

The mill wasn't running. Charlie had talked to her insurance agent and he had told her to leave everything untouched until an adjuster could make an inspection. She'd been promised a man would be there that afternoon, but in the meantime the crew had an unscheduled day off. She expected the sheriff to come along at any time, too, and right this minute she wasn't overly thrilled at having to channel her thoughts into an interview.

But Joan Summers was here . . . and hopeful. "Come into my office, Joan," Charlie invited, leading the way.

Half an hour later McAllister Lumber Company had a new employee. Joan had an excellent background, with experience in a sawmill office much like Charlie's. Cole had been right to insist on his personnel manager getting into the search for the right person, but Charlie was too weighted down with other matters to either applaud or begrudge Cole's foresight. In truth, when she thought of Cole, within the muddle of all the problems besieging her, it was to acknowledge again and puzzle over what she had finally admitted last night: she liked him.

Cole was like no man she'd ever known. He reached something in her that had barely been tapped before, a womanly need, a wanting, and not just a physical wanting, although there was no doubt he also strongly affected her sexually. It occurred to Charlie that Cole was the kind of man she'd been waiting for all of her adult life. She wondered if it were possible that she'd turned away from lesser relationships in the past because she'd somehow known there was such a man out there somewhere.

If that were the case, how ironic it was that the man who fit what she really wanted out of life was also a man she didn't trust. That thought was the repeated conclusion to a circle that covered every moment she and Cole Morgan had spent together; it gave Charlie a sick feeling every time she reached it. She was in an emotional quandary where Cole was concerned, seared with memories that encompassed passion, resentment and anger. He drew emotion from her so easily, she realized, too easily. When had she last lost her temper like she had with him? Or when had she last been so painfully ambivalent about something, whether it be a person or a completely intangible subject?

Admitting she liked Cole Morgan had accomplished nothing, certainly nothing in Charlie's favor. She was still who she was, as was Cole. Nothing had magically changed just because she had undergone a burst of enlightenment.

Well, that wasn't entirely true. One change was noticeable, but it wasn't one she enjoyed—a strange sense of sadness. Normally a pretty upbeat person, Charlie recognized a melancholy that was completely foreign to her personality. What's more, she didn't know how to get rid of it.

THE FOURTH OF JULY was on a Friday, making a three-day holiday, and Charlie looked forward to Cassie coming home. Other than brief meetings in Missoula when Charlie was there on business, the sisters had seen little of each other for months. Gibbs always went all out for the Fourth, celebrating with a parade, games and picnics in the park and fireworks after dark. It was the little town's one big effort each year and almost everyone in the Three Forks area participated.

Joan was working out so well, Charlie wondered how she had struggled along without office help for so long. The days had settled into a productive routine, and by the time the holiday came around, the trauma of the two fires had diminished from fearful disbelief to tolerability.

It wasn't until Cassie and Jim Heath had arrived late Thursday afternoon and the three of them were chatting over coffee, though, that Charlie realized how passively she was accepting the agreement with Cole. First, she told her sister and Jim about the fires. Cassie knew they had occurred, of course, but was anxious to discuss them in greater detail than phone conversation had allowed.

Once that topic was behind them they talked about the contract with Canfield Lumber Company, and that's when Charlie privately admitted she had changed a great deal in the past few weeks. Without a concern for timber keeping her worked up as it had for so long, she had drifted into a day-by-day complacency, concentrating on increased production in the mill rather than staying alert for the opportunity to reclaim her independence.

Both Cassie and Jim's opinion was that she was in an enviable position with the contract, but Charlie experienced a weakening self-disloyalty while they discussed it. How had she become so placid over something so important? How could she have forgotten in such a short time that she was no longer in command of her own ship?

The whole subject made her uneasy and Charlie veered from it, turning the direction of conversation to Jim. As Cassie had proclaimed so often, Jim was an impressive man. Very good-looking with sandy hair and brown eyes, he radiated intelligence and good taste, and Charlie found herself liking him and understanding her sister's infatuation. It was apparent the attraction was mutual, and Charlie had a feeling these two were headed for something serious.

The thought brought Cole to mind, reawakening the stinging sadness Charlie felt so much of the time. She'd heard nothing from Cole since the second fire, which, after the concern and tenderness he'd shown her that night, surprised her a little. It shouldn't, she told herself. He was only doing what she'd asked from the beginning—maintaining their relationship on a strictly business level.

Thursday evening Cassie and Charlie fried two-dozen chickens, made gallons of potato and macaroni salads and organized boxes of condiments. Traditionally the wives of the mill crew brought desserts and the McAllisters had always provided the fried chicken, cold beer and soft drinks. Jim helped where he could, but it was midnight before everything was ready and they could go to bed.

Charlie awoke at dawn the next morning, showered and dressed in a white sundress and went downstairs to begin the day. The annual picnic was always fun, but this year her heart just wasn't in it.

Would Cole take part in the festivities? Had he moved into his new house yet? Would they run into each other today? Would he even care if they did?

Maybe he had left the area for the long weekend. Some people did.

Sighing, Charlie made coffee and started breakfast. And when Jim and Cassie joined her in the kitchen, neither of them could tell that behind Charlie's smile beat a heavy heart.

IT WAS EARLY EVENING before Charlie had a moment to catch her breath. The day had been packed full of friends and conversation, too much food and lots of laughter, and while it had been tiring, it had succeeded in lifting Charlie's spirits. Cassie and Jim had gone to watch the final inning of a softball game, and Charlie and a group of women had put the few leftovers away.

With the picnic breaking up, Charlie strolled around the park, stopping to speak to friends now and then. It occurred to her, as she wandered aimlessly, that she might be looking for Cole, hoping for an opportunity to speak to him, maybe just to see what reaction seeing her might arouse . . . if any. She was in a strange mood, she knew, one that had gotten hold of her the night of the fire and had pervaded her periodically ever since.

Part of it was loneliness, Charlie realized, surprising herself. Was that possible? Solitude had never bothered her. She had always been so content with the mill, busy with a dozen different thoughts at the same time. But it wasn't enough anymore. There was a yearning inside her, a need, a dissatisfaction, and the components of life that had once been so fulfilling were no longer enough.

Walking in a circle, Charlie ended up back at the picnic site. Jim and Cassie were waiting for her. Cassie's eyes sparkled as she told Charlie of the plans she had made with the friends they'd run into. They had agreed to meet at the Buckhorn, a popular local bar and dance hall, after the fireworks. "Will you come along?"

It had been ages since Charlie had danced, and there wasn't any point in clinging to wistful thoughts of Cole. He hadn't come to the park and there was no telling what he'd done for the holiday. "Thanks, I'd like to come," she said, smiling.

WHILE CHARLIE CHANGED clothes and got ready for the Buckhorn later, she realized how fortunate she was she hadn't run across Cole that day. With her unusual, moody loneliness, she suspected she could have easily fallen into something with him, had he pressed her again. It was best they stay completely apart.

Her priorities were aligning again, and nothing really had changed. She was working for Cole and she didn't like it. Next week she would definitely get back to what was important: finding a way to function independently again. There had to be a way, she just hadn't found it yet.

It was Jim who ultimately gave her the idea. It was during the drive to the Buckhorn. "That section of land you and Cassie own, Charlie, Cassie tells me you've logged it."

"That's right," Charlie said. "I had to, or close the doors of the mill a year ago."

"So I understand. But Cassie, you said it had a great fishing stream, didn't you?"

"Oh, it does," Cassie enthused. "Dad always claimed he had the biggest and best trout in the state right there on our own land."

Charlie detected more in Jim's tone than his words implied. "What are you getting at, Jim?"

"Well, I'm no expert, of course. But it seems to me with that kind of fishing, some dedicated angler might love to get his hands on that property. Have you thought about selling it?"

Charlie and Cassie both nodded, and Charlie replied, "I had it appraised. With the timber gone, we wouldn't get very much for it."

"Then what about a trade?"

"A trade?" both women echoed.

"Yes, a trade. Trade your section of logged-off fishing land for a smaller piece with timber."

"My Lord," Charlie murmured huskily, startled by the

full meaning of Jim's suggestion. That's what she'd been overlooking all this time, and it had taken an outsider to see it.

7

THE BUCKHORN'S PARKING LOT was overflowing with cars and pickups. Jim finally located a space a good hike from the front door, and even at that distance the country band, loud laughter and voices from the night spot could be heard.

Charlie and Cassie knew they were probably acquainted with most of the people within the squat, rambling log building, and anticipating dancing and laughing with old friends was like a tonic. With Cassie holding Jim's hand, the three of them ran through the parking lot.

"Everyone in the county must be here," Cassie shouted gaily above the din as they squeezed through the crowd just inside the door.

Hellos were called out and smiles exchanged while Cassie scanned the throng for the friends they were to meet. She spotted them at a large table and waved. "There they are," she exclaimed, and led the way through the mass.

Faces blurred until Charlie was seated. Then she looked around at the people on the dance floor and crowding the other tables. Rick Slaughter was at the bar, Pete and Mave were dancing and Joan Summers was with a group at a table some distance away. Joan waved and Charlie waved back, then continued her visual journey about the dimly lit room.

She felt something suddenly prickle her spine. Cole was at a table with six people Charlie didn't know and appeared to be having a very good time, laughing, talking, drinking beer. Charlie found herself staring. Without a doubt he was the best-looking man in the place, and even across yards and yards of moving bodies, she felt Cole's pull. He wasn't looking her way, and Charlie took the moment to indulge in a long, uninterrupted study.

He was only the most devastating-looking man she'd ever seen, she decided with the intensity of feeling she was no longer trying to deny. Everyone was in jeans and boots; people didn't come to the Buckhorn in anything but jeans and boots, and only shirts and blouses varied the uniform. Women wore brightly colored summer tops, men wore Western shirts, and more than a few heads in the crowd were topped with big hats. The scene was typically Montanan—casual attire, congenial atmosphere. Yet, in all that uniformity of clothing and attitude, Cole stood out.

For everyone . . . or just for her?

Charlie stirred, bringing her attention back to the table. Glasses of beer were being poured from pitchers, and everyone seemed to be talking at once. Someone asked her to dance, and she got up with a smile.

The music was terrific—played by an exceptionally good country band that had been imported for the holiday weekend—and Charlie was enjoying herself more than she had in aeons. She danced three numbers in a row then begged off the next, declaring she needed a break. Sipping some beer to ease her parched throat, she was immediately drawn into the bantering crowd again.

"Hello, Charlie."

There was no mistaking the voice. She turned, knowing instantly she'd been hoping for this. "Hello, Cole." Jim and Cassie were dancing, but Charlie quickly made introductions to the others at the table. She could see a light in some of her friends' eyes, one that said, "So, this is the great Cole Morgan!"

"Join us," a few of them called.

Cole smiled. "Thanks, but my family is here with me. Charlie, would you like to dance?"

A fast song was just winding down and Charlie knew the next one would be a slow number. The band had unfailingly alternated lively tunes with slow, dreamy numbers, and it looked like Cole had timed his invitation to coincide with the latter.

Something warm and alive was developing in Charlie's breast—the response to this man she was so powerless to control. Perversely, she welcomed it, still afraid to explore it but finding it strangely more satisfying than the uneasy loneliness she'd been living with. She put her hand in Cole's and stood up with a murmured "Yes."

There were the few minutes between songs to get through. Cole steered her through the crush of people leaving the dance floor and those arriving with the same intent as they, to dance to the upcoming slow beat. "How've you been?" Cole asked.

"Well, thank you. And you?"

"Good enough, I guess."

They were talking, exchanging pleasantries as though they were ordinary acquaintances. Was it possible to dance with this man and relax within the circle of his arms? To just forget everything else and enjoy the tingling excitement she felt deep inside her?

The band struck a note and the lights came down. Cole took her hands and slowly brought her forward, and then they were dancing, moving in unison to the music. He took small steps, he moved smoothly, he smelled divine, and he felt like no one Charlie had ever danced with before.

There were several topics either of them could have opened a conversation with, but neither did it. They were only dancing a few moments before Cole wound her left hand behind her waist and drew her into a more intimate position. Her breasts touched his chest, her thighs moved with his. As if in a dream, Charlie followed Cole's lead, totally immersed in the beautiful sensation of dancing with a man whose very nearness fired her senses.

She could feel his heartbeat against her. His closeness was intoxicating. Charlie felt it happening to Cole, too. His shirt was suddenly softer, the flesh beneath it molding to her own body. She grew breathless, flushed and became more so when he spoke huskily in her ear. "You look beautiful tonight, Charlie."

"Thank you," she whispered.

After circling the floor, Cole tilted his head back and smiled at her. "Did you have a nice holiday?"

Charlie drew a much-needed breath. "Very nice. My sister and a friend came for the weekend. The Fourth is always the annual company picnic. Did I hear you say your family is here, too?"

"Yes. They came for a combination housewarming and holiday."

"Then you've moved in?"

"A week ago. The decorator is hard at work, by the way."

Charlie smiled. "With what colors?"

"Not purple." Cole laughed. "Would you come over to the table and meet the gang later?"

"Meet your family?" Charlie asked, not trying to hide her surprise.

"I'd like you to, if you wouldn't mind."

"I wouldn't mind at all, but . . ."

"Good."

When that was settled, Cole bent his head again and spoke softly against her cheek, "You feel so right in my arms. Are you still dead set against anything personal between us?"

She felt choked. "I . . . I wish things were different," she managed, knowing it was a rather obscure reply.

"Different, how?"

"Just . . . different."

Cole looked at her, searching her green eyes and seeing her meaning quite clearly. Her desire to have things "different" was heartwarming—an admission that she'd been thinking of him as more than the other signature on their contract. "If things were different, we'd be a lot more than friends, wouldn't we?"

Charlie looked away. He was so direct. Yet how could she deny what he'd said when every cell in her body was longing for him? He had to feel it, just as she felt his response. "I . . . suppose so."

"You know it as well as I do. I'm not giving up on us, Charlie. I can't. Look, I've got my family here, but they wouldn't mind going back to the house without me later. Let me drive you home so we can talk. Please don't say no."

Emotions warred. She liked him, she feared him, she wanted to say yes, she was afraid to. Her own mood was dangerous. Talk about what?

Oh, what a dumb question. Talk about them, naturally. Talk about why they shouldn't be anything they wanted to be—friends, lovers, business associates.

Did she want to dissect it again? To enumerate her doubts again?

Charlie swallowed the lump in her throat. It was so hard to think with her breasts pressed to his chest. He must feel her nipples. She knew they were aroused, just as he was. Oh, yes, there was no ignoring the most manly part of him, not with it searing her through two layers of denim.

She sighed. Maybe, just maybe, she wouldn't list all the reasons why things couldn't possibly progress for them again. Maybe she should try to separate business and pleasure, as he apparently was doing. Right at this moment she didn't feel lonely, did she?

The music stopped and the lights came up. Couples who had been cuddling broke apart and Charlie waited for Cole to move away. But he didn't, he just kept holding her. "Let me drive you home," he repeated urgently.

She could see over Cole's shoulder that people were watching. Cassie, especially, looked abnormally curious. "Yes," Charlie whispered quickly. "All right, you may drive me home."

Cole smiled and stepped back. He took her hand. "Come and meet my rowdy family."

Nervous over the prospect, wondering why he was insisting, Charlie allowed herself to be led through the crowd. Three men stood up as they approached Cole's table. "Charlie, this is Marion, my sister . . ."

Cole named all six people around the table and Charlie memorized names to faces as he spoke. "Everyone, this is Charlotte McAllister, better known as Charlie."

Everyone was cordial and asked her to sit down. "For a few minutes," she agreed, taking the chair Cole pulled out for her.

One of Cole's brothers, Brady, spoke up. "I understand you're in the lumber business, too."

"Why . . . yes." Surprised that Cole had mentioned her beforehand, Charlie glanced his way. She saw a strangely proud expression on his face, as though he had praised her in advance and was enjoying his family's curiosity. "Of course, my mill isn't in the same league with Cole's," she added.

"Charlie's plant is a tight little operation," Cole boasted. "And incidentally, Charlie, the lumber I've been getting from you is A1."

"Thank you." Charlie was amazed that she, too, felt pride. Where was the old resentment she'd always felt when she put Cole and business together? There hadn't been a drop of patronization in Cole's flattery and the handsome Morgan family were all beaming at her, as though welcoming her into their ranks. It was a rather odd situation.

But, remembering her own family at the Buckhorn, Charlie stayed seated only a few more minutes. Rising, she smiled around the table. "It was very nice meeting all of you," she exclaimed, and turned to Cole. "I really must get back to Cassie and Jim."

"I'll walk you back," Cole said, and again they wound through the crowd.

Cassie's eyes were wide when they approached, and after another set of introductions and Cole had gone, she whispered teasingly, "Seems like you've been holding back a rather important fact about Mr. Cole Morgan, sis. He's quite nice-looking, isn't he?"

It was funny how Cassie's observation struck Charlie. Nice-looking? Cole? He was only the greatest-looking man she'd ever seen. Did Cassie see him as only "nice" looking?

Charlie fought the impulse to ask her sister if she thought Jim Heath was better-looking and laughed instead, already positive what Cassie would say. Hormones did funny things to people, and indeed, beauty was in the eye of the beholder. Cole was gaining quite a reputation in the community, with even Mave Dirksen labeling him a "handsome devil." Even so, Cassie was so smitten with Jim, she probably thought male charm only came with sandy hair and brown eyes.

For herself, Charlie acknowledged in a flash of complete honesty, it came with black hair, blue eyes and a tall, imposing carriage.

For the remainder of the evening, every time Charlie thought of her promise to ride home with Cole, her heart fluttered alarmingly. Was she playing with fire?

At that inane question she merely shook her head. Of course she was playing with fire. But it was a flame she was presently of a mind to challenge, she realized. All that had happened since she'd met Cole had led up to this moment. Her hormones were demanding something, too, just as Cassie's were. Charlie was tense, keyed up, and every fiber of her being was tuned to one person in the overcrowded club—Cole Morgan.

After midnight the crowd began to thin out, and by closing time the Buckhorn looked like it did on an ordinary night. This had been a bang-up party, a climax to a fun-filled Fourth of July, and must have been a profitable night for the club's owners, Charlie mused. She hadn't told Cassie about riding home with Cole yet, but as the group around the table began to gather up purses and talk about leaving, Charlie knew it was time to do so.

She nudged her sister. "Cass, Cole asked to drive me home. Do you mind?"

Cassie looked at Jim, then grinned at Charlie. "What do you think?"

Charlie laughed. "I think you don't mind," she retorted dryly.

Cole was walking toward them. Cassie leaned closer and whispered, "He really is good-looking, sis. Have fun."

"Ready to go?" Cole asked with a broad smile.

"Sure am." Charlie got up and said good-night to everyone. With Cole's hand warm and possessive on her arm as they traversed the club to the door, Charlie knew this exit wasn't going unnoticed. Tomorrow it would be all over Gibbs and the Three Forks area that Charlie McAllister had left the Buckhorn with Cole Morgan.

That was the way of a community where everyone knew everyone else. For the most part Charlie liked the camaraderie of such familiarity. It was pleasant and satisfying to live among people she knew so well, but there were moments, like now, when a little anonymity would have been welcome.

Cole brought her to his car. "How will your family get home?" Charlie asked as she slid onto the Lincoln's luxurious seat.

"We have two cars here. They can all squeeze into one for the trip back," he explained, closing the passenger door.

It seemed strange and yet perfectly natural, both at the same time, to be in Cole's car. He got in and closed his door, and at once the interior of the car became warmer. The motor purred to life. "Hungry?" he asked as he drove from the parking lot onto the highway. "We could stop at Potter's for something to eat."

Eating wasn't on Charlie's mind. For one thing she was too nervous to even consider eating. For another, she had already eaten so much picnic fare that day, she might not be hungry again for a week. And walking into Potter's Café, the only all-night restaurant in the Three Forks area, with Cole just wasn't in her plans. No doubt half of the revelers from the Buckhorn had recongregated at Potter's, and she'd provided enough fodder for the gossip mill for one evening.

"I'm not the least bit hungry," she answered firmly.

"I'd like some coffee. I'll run in and get some to go. How's that?"

"That's fine."

She'd been right, Charlie saw when the Lincoln stopped at Potter's Café. The place was packed. "Be back in a minute," Cole said.

It took at least ten minutes, but finally he came back with two large Styrofoam containers of coffee. There was a cup holder on the console of the car and Cole placed the cups in it.

When they were in motion again Cole laughed. "Do you realize we have no place to go? You have company and my house is overfull. Six adults and seven children take up a lot of space."

"Seven children?"

"Brady and Don each have three and Marion has one. She's expecting again, though, so in about six months there'll be eight. Prolific bunch, huh?"

"They all seem very nice."

"They are. I've got a great family." Cole shot her a glance. "Your sister seems nice, too."

"Cassie's the best," Charlie proclaimed sincerely.

"It's great that she came."

"Yes. This is the first weekend she's had off in ages. Cass is working two jobs this summer." Charlie shied away from giving him the reason for the second job, but made a mental note to talk to her sister about it. With the mill running steadily now, it wasn't necessary for Cassie to drain herself with two jobs.

Charlie could see where Cole was heading, down to the river. There were quiet, isolated spots along the river for talking privately, and it was also the local teenagers' favorite parking area.

But they had to stop somewhere, and as Cole had pointed out, both of their homes were full of guests. Maybe that was best. Considering the odd mood she'd been in lately, there was no telling what direction their conversation might take.

Charlie squirmed with a touch of anxiety. What was she expecting from this? Why had she even agreed?

Was it simply that she wanted to spend time with Cole?

When had she become so ambivalent, running hot and cold toward a situation? She'd always been so direct, as direct as she felt Cole to be, but even the most generous opinion of her recent behavior couldn't construe it as direct.

The Lincoln came to a halt along the riverbank. Cole killed the engine and rolled his window down. Immediately the chirps of crickets and the burble of the slowly moving water drifted in. "Great night," Cole said quietly.

Charlie unhooked her seat belt and leaned her head back. She was here—for who knew what reason—and it really was very pleasant. How many years had it been since she'd sat by this river with a man? Actually, it was so long ago, the "man" had been a boy—and the memory made Charlie smile. "We have so few really warm nights here, they're always a treat," she agreed.

"Here, have your coffee." Cole handed her a cup.

"Thanks."

A comfortable silence ensued. Everything seemed oddly right with the world at the moment, Charlie reflected. It was an extraordinary feeling, a rare feeling, and caused by being with this man on such a beautiful night. She had stopped denying she liked Cole, but still, how did he have the power to make even a quiet moment like this so meaningful?

Turning in the seat so his back was to the door, Cole asked softly, "How should we begin, Charlie?"

Uh-oh. Now it would come. And was she prepared for it, whatever "it" was? Charlie gave a small, unsteady laugh. "Maybe I'll leave that up to you."

"All right." Cole spoke thoughtfully. "I wonder how blunt I dare be."

"Uh . . . blunt?" Now what did he mean by that?

"Yes, blunt. I have a feeling you'd appreciate and understand a straightforward approach. Am I wrong?"

Charlie sipped her coffee, stalling for time. A straightforward approach? How straightforward? She could only reply to such a loaded question one way. "I think that depends on the subject matter, Cole."

"I think we both know what the subject is. I haven't been able to get those minutes in my house out of my mind. Do you have any idea how many women I've met around here since I bought Canfield? No, you couldn't know. Well, it's a pretty high number. By the same token, you couldn't know how many of them made the slightest impression. There's been only one, Charlie, a tall, beautiful, green-eyed sawmill owner. You."

Charlie had literally stopped breathing. To hear such a thing from a man of Cole's stature, to hear that he regarded her so highly, had indeed taken her breath away. Her heart thudded in her chest while she sought a reply.

But Cole didn't wait for an answer. "I want you, Charlie. I want your friendship and I want you. I want us to see each other. I want us to have evenings together, weekends . . ."

Oh, dear God, this was too much too soon! And dare she believe him? She was at risk here, more than she'd ever been in her life. Her own vulnerability frightened her. "Cole! Please, you're moving too fast."

"Am I? All right, I'll slow down. But I'm sure you get my drift. I have a lot of feelings for you, Charlie, feelings that I want to explore. I'd like to see where they might lead. I think that kiss we shared was just the tip of something so special we'd be fools to keep on pretending it didn't happen. And we're not fools, either of us," he added after a brief pause. "Now . . . tell me what you think about all this."

Charlie stared out the window, watching touches of silver play across the surface of the dark river water. How should she answer? How could it be so simple for him? For her there was such a complexity of interwoven feelings.

Liking him didn't dissolve the reality of their situation, even if it was blurring it unmercifully. "I'm confused, Cole," she murmured huskily.

"Because you like me and you don't want to?"

Oh, Lord, he was perceptive. He was so full of disarming traits, taking her by surprise again and again. "Something like that," she admitted, again in that throaty voice.

Cole finished his coffee and put the empty cup back in the holder. His arm stretched across the seat back and he took her braid gently. "The night of the fire, when your hair was loose, you were so beautiful, Charlie."

She closed her eyes for a moment, allowing a lovely warmth to gather through her. His touch was magic, a delight so welcome she wondered if it was why she was here. Could she be honest enough to admit such a thing, even to herself? Cole had been that honest, stating positively that he hadn't been able to forget the kiss. Well, had she forgotten it?

A blindingly startling thought followed: was she falling in love with Cole Morgan? This wasn't just playing with fire, was it? It was leaping headfirst into an inferno.

She was in such a frame of mind, one that almost dared fate. She was an adult, the only person in the entire world she had to explain anything to, and right now she wanted Cole to touch her. Did she need a long, complicated excuse for that?

Cole stirred. He was picking up something from Charlie that made his pulse race. It was a wordless communication, a silent message, and he was sure he was reading it right. Without hesitation he eased across the seat, took the cup from her hands and put it in the holder next to his.

In the next instant his arms were around her, his face buried in her throat. "Don't keep fighting me," he whispered, his lips burning a path to her mouth.

His kiss was hungry, demanding a response, which he got almost instantly as Charlie's soul was reaching out to him, and the nagging, unsettled feelings that were still a part of her were quickly losing significance. She could only kiss him back, lift her arms to his neck and press into his strength.

His lips weren't gentle. They were rough, writhing, inflaming, and she wished him closer—closer than was possible with clothing and the restraint of their position. My Lord, what she wanted from him, what she needed so badly was . . .

"Charlie . . ." Cole's voice was guttural, gruff, it was a hoarse cry of pleasure at her passionate response. His mouth descended again, and while his tongue hotly probed, his hand roamed. She felt exquisite—firm, curving flesh, breasts that were a delicious handful, a waist that was a mere handspan.

Her cream-colored knit blouse contained small pearl buttons from a slightly scooped neckline to a ribbed waistband, and with one arm around her neck and their lips locked in a soul-searing kiss, Cole undid them. One by one. It was an exercise of will to do it so slowly when what he wanted was to rip the offending garment from her. In all of his adult life he'd never experienced a hotter, more urgent desire to see and touch a woman's bare breasts.

Her breath was coming in short gasps and his was shattering the night quiet. A part of Cole's brain was exultant. He'd known it would be wild between them; he'd known that since their first kiss. He wanted her desperately, but to know, to feel she wanted him the same way was even more erotically exciting.

At last the blouse was unbuttoned and he pushed it open, lifting his head to see what beauty he'd uncovered. Her bra was the color of her skin, a delicate ivory, a garment that was visible more from its satiny fabric than by its color. He brought his face down to the sweetly scented cleavage of her breasts and inhaled her lush femaleness.

Dazed, Charlie felt him reach behind her and unhook the band of her bra. Her understanding of his need developed along with a need of her own to see and touch Cole in the same way. Her fingers rose to his shirtfront, and it was easily opened for it had snaps. She laughed softly as they popped apart, but Cole hardly noticed. And then she didn't notice much else, either, not when she felt his mouth on one of her nipples.

"Ohh," she moaned softly as his tongue circled and teased.

"You're beautiful . . . so beautiful," he rasped. "Charlie, I want you."

"I know," she whispered, closing her eyes to the incredible torment he was creating.

The next instant, her eyes opened, wide and startled. Cole was sitting up straight and arranging her clothing. "But not here," he said grimly. "Our first time together isn't going to be in the front seat of a car. Is your sister leaving Sunday?"

Charlie tried to understand, to calm herself. "Yes, Sunday."

"So is my family. Whose house, Charlie, yours or mine? You choose, but on Sunday . . ."

Sunday, the day after tomorrow. No, that was a mistake. If she had time to think she would back out.

Wouldn't she?

Charlie sat back weakly. What *would* she do on Sunday?

8

SATURDAY WAS SPENT in lazy relaxation. A hammock in the backyard was used often throughout the day; they ate picnic leftovers whenever they were hungry, and all in all, Charlie, Cassie and Jim had a comfortable, easy day.

If it weren't for what tomorrow was bringing, Charlie would have enjoyed the carefree hours immensely. Actually, whenever Sunday sneaked into her mind, she forcibly threw it out. She couldn't allow herself to think about it. Not yet.

Cassie asked about Cole, of course, and Charlie hedged so blatantly that her sister raised an inquisitive eyebrow and laughed.

Their one serious conversation was about Cassie's plans. "I can afford to help you with school again, Cass, and I wish you would quit one of your jobs."

Cassie shook her head adamantly. "No, Charlie. I'll need the bookstore job again this fall and severing ties with a good part-time job isn't sensible. As for the bank, I really like working there. Besides," she added with a twinkling excitement in her lovely blue-gray eyes. "I want to keep working with Jim."

Charlie studied her sister. "Are you falling in love?"

A thoughtful look sobered Cassie's pretty face. "I could be. I know I care about Jim a great deal."

"Well, he's a nice guy, Cass. But you wouldn't let that interfere with your last year of college, would you?"

Cassie gave a startled laugh. "I haven't even given that a thought. Let's just wait and see what happens, sis. There are times when I might do anything if Jim crooked his little finger."

Seeing Charlie's disapproving expression, Cassie added hastily, "Don't worry. He hasn't crooked his finger . . . yet."

After a long and restless night, Charlie waved Cassie and Jim off just before noon on Sunday. Then she went back into the house, grim over the decision she could no longer put off.

A series of alternatives passed through her mind. She could leave the house and go somewhere, anywhere; she could ignore the phone or the door, should Cole come around; or, of course, she could simply tell him she wasn' interested.

Which was a lie. She *was* interested, so overwhelmingly interested it frightened her. When had she ever been more interested in a man? In making love with him? In being a part of everything his kisses promised?

Her body burned every time she let Friday night into her thoughts, and now that she was alone and unable to force her attention elsewhere, it was riveted inwardly, on herself, on inner demands she was scarcely able to believe.

Yet wasn't it rather cold-blooded to be planning a meeting to make love? There was no mistaking Cole's intentions. If they had been in more comfortable surroundings Friday night, they would already have made love. But it would have been spontaneous. This wasn't spontaneous, this was an insensitive, deliberate action, and one she knew she should avoid.

"Damn," Charlie muttered at intervals for the next two hours.

Despite the flutterings of common sense, though, Charlie knew she was waiting for the phone to ring. And she'd

done special things to herself, such as fluff drying her hair
after a shampoo and leaving it loose rather than braiding
it, and picking a pretty blue-and-white sundress to wear,
both efforts solely because she thought Cole would admire
her in a dress with her hair down.

Charlie paced. Why was she doing this? What would
come after?

Oh, she was taking such a big bite. Would she regret it?

IT WAS A LONG DRIVE back to Oregon for Cole's family, and
they left early Sunday morning. Because of the long weekend away from his office, Cole spent a few hours there, but
he didn't get a whole lot done. Charlie kept coming between him and whatever he tried to read, and he finally gave
up on the hope of accomplishing anything and left.

There had been moments during the pleasant Saturday
with his brothers and sister, their spouses and children when
Cole wondered if he hadn't made the blunder of the century Friday night. It wouldn't have been the first time he'd
had sex in a car, and he kept trying to figure out why it
hadn't felt right with Charlie. All he knew was he wanted
her beyond anything he could have dreamed up, but he
wanted her in a bed, where he could undo that braid and
see that golden mane on a pillow and he could take his time
and undress her slowly.

A quickie encounter on a car seat wasn't enough, not near
enough, and it also wasn't good enough for Charlie. There
was something very special about his feelings for her,
something he couldn't put a name to, but he knew it was
different than anything he'd ever experienced before.

Still, the timing had been right Friday night, and she'd
been willing and eager and he'd let it slip away. In retro-
spect he cursed his sudden attack of high-mindedness,

worrying that the hours since might have eroded the passion Charlie had been so caught up in.

It sure hadn't eroded his. All he could think of was Charlie, and it was all he could do to wait until midafternoon to call her.

When the phone finally rang in the McAllister household, Charlie jumped a foot. She stared at it through four rings, then walked over and picked it up self-consciously, her heart in her throat. "Hello?"

Her voice went right through Cole. "How are you, Charlie?"

She sat down weakly, wincing at the familiarity in Cole's voice. "I'm all right."

"Has your sister gone?"

"Yes."

A low chuckle preceded "So has my bunch. It was great seeing them, but I sure had a time yesterday keeping my mind on track. I kept thinking about today."

Charlie swallowed hard. "Me, too, Cole . . . about today . . ."

Damn! What he'd feared had happened. She was back to where they'd been before Friday night. Cole interrupted, pretending not to catch the doubt he heard. "Do you want to come here, or shall I go there?"

He heard Charlie take a sharp breath. He would have to go easy. She was wary, uncertain. "Charlie, I don't plan to force you into anything."

"But . . ."

"I just want to see you. I promise not to pressure you."

"Cole . . . I don't know . . ."

"Please don't say no. Why don't you come here? In fact, let me come and pick you up. I've got steaks in the freezer and all the fixin's for a salad. We'll cook dinner together. How about it?"

Had she read more into Friday night than she should have? Charlie frowned while she thought about it. No, she'd understood Cole perfectly, just as she'd understood what had been happening to herself. Only today, he was smart enough to sense she was having second thoughts.

Well, she did believe he wouldn't do anything she wasn't in favor of, so it would really be up to her, wouldn't it? And somehow his changing the emphasis of the date made it a lot more acceptable. At least they could pretend they wanted to eat together and see what happened.

"All right. But you needn't come and get me. I'd rather drive myself." Then she could always leave, she added privately.

"Great. You won't be long, will you?"

"About an hour."

"I'll take the steaks out of the freezer. See you soon."

WHEN CHARLIE GOT TO COLE'S she was still in the sundress. But her hair was drawn back into the familiar French braid and she felt much more comfortable with the controlled style.

Cole had been watching for her and came out of the house before her pickup stopped. He opened her door and smiled, determined to put her at ease. "Hi," he said, taking her hand to assist her out.

"Hi." Charlie jumped the long step from truck to ground. "I see you're having some landscaping done."

"Come take a look." Holding her hand casually, Cole walked her around the yard and pointed out various newly planted shrubs and trees. "I don't want too much done," he explained. "I'd rather maintain a natural look."

"I agree. This is a lovely spot. It doesn't need a lot of extras."

"Come inside. I think you're going to like the house now."

"I'm sure I will." She sounded so calm, Charlie commended herself.

They entered and Charlie stopped, amazed at the change furniture and carpeting made. "Oh, Cole, it's beautiful," she breathed.

"And blue," he laughed.

The carpeting was a soft blue, but blue nonetheless, and Charlie gave him a teasing glance. "I think you knew it would be blue all along."

"Probably," Cole conceded. "I've got some wine chilling. Make yourself at home while I get it."

Charlie walked over to the living-room windows, marveling at the view while she waited. She was here and nothing felt too amiss. Cole was glad to see her, she could tell that, but it only gave her a welcome feeling, nothing to worry about.

Besides, maybe she wasn't going to worry anyway. Cole looked gorgeous in white jeans and a navy-blue shirt. His house was fabulous and the day was young. Who knew what might happen? Or what she might do when it did?

Lord, she was bold lately!

Well, *lately* was a misnomer. She'd never been a shrinking violet, had she? And if she was struck down tomorrow with the enormity of complicating an intolerable business situation with a romantic involvement, what then?

This coming week, probably tomorrow, she was going to try Jim Heath's suggestion. She would call the realtors in the area and ask them to list her section of land as a trade.

What if it worked? What if it actually got results?

She wasn't thrilled with their business arrangement, and Cole knew it. But would he be upset if she should terminate it?

Frowning, Charlie mulled it over. He'd agreed to the thirty-day clause, but she had a feeling he was rather complacent about the whole thing, as though she'd given up on running independently again. And could she blame him? Had she done anything in the last few weeks to make him think otherwise?

Cole returned with a bottle of wine in an ice bucket and two stemmed glasses. "What have you heard from your insurance company on the fire loss, Charlie?" he asked while uncorking the wine.

She joined him at the low table situated between lovely blue brocade couches in front of the fireplace. "They're talking about a settlement. It's quite an involved procedure, or at least they're making it involved."

Cole filled the glasses. "Then they're planning to honor the claim?"

"I think so. I had an adjuster in the office for a whole day last week going through my records. The company wants the exact cost of producing the lumber lost. As for the profit I would have made, forget it. Cost is all they're concerned with."

"Sounds standard. I was afraid they wouldn't pay anything with the fire being a deliberate act of arson."

Charlie accepted a glass of wine and sat on one of the couches. "There seems to be a modicum of doubt about that, Cole. That gas can gave everyone ideas, but they haven't been able to prove it wasn't left there accidentally. Frankly, I don't know what to think. I can't imagine a fire getting started out there without some help."

"I agree." Cole sat on the opposite couch. "Well, it's not like it was a million-dollar claim. Maybe they didn't put a lot of time on it."

"That's possible," Charlie agreed.

Cole smiled at her. "You look nice in here, just like you belong."

She laughed. "Probably because of this blue-and-white dress."

"Which, incidentally, is very pretty. I like you in dresses."

"Thanks." How nice they were being! Only one thing prevented the scene from being genuinely humdrum, a barely noticeable cast in Cole's eyes. He was waiting, Charlie realized, biding his time, content to play the game for as long as she wanted.

She felt a nervous laugh bubble up in her throat and stifled it with another swallow of wine. Whatever this was, whatever it became, it wasn't a laughing matter. Cole had more power in his smile alone than any other man she'd ever known had had in his entire bag of tricks. And wasn't that the heart of the excitement Cole created—the power of a drugging smile and the fact that she knew she shouldn't like him and did anyway? What was that old saying about forbidden fruit being the sweetest?

Cole got up and turned on the stereo, and when he sat again he chose the same couch Charlie was using. She smiled and immediately wondered if she'd been wrong in assuming he was willing to play an indefinite waiting game.

But he merely sat back comfortably, resting one arm along the top of the couch, not even touching her. Charlie relaxed in her corner, especially when Cole began talking about his family's visit. Even so, odd thoughts drifted through her mind behind the suitable replies she made.

Was their casual conversation phony? Were they suddenly going to stop all pretense and leap at each other? Friday night was in the air, no matter how many laughs they shared over anecdotes about his nieces and nephews.

Finally, after two glasses of wine and an hour of seemingly innocent sociability, Cole put his glass down and stood up. There was an endless tape of soft background music coming from unseen stereo speakers, and he held his hand out. "Dance with me, Charlie."

Her heart jumped. "Dance?"

"Yes. Like we did Friday night. Remember?"

"Of course I remember. But here? On this blue carpet?"

Cole waggled his eyebrows humorously. "Haven't you ever heard of 'cutting a rug'?"

"What?" Charlie was so startled by the silly little joke, she burst out laughing. Cole wasn't a man who made jokes every few minutes, which was another thing she liked about him. Jokes were fun, but one time she'd dated a man who'd been a continual joker and it had palled very quickly. Sometimes, though, a light attitude was great, like right now. It not only brought a laugh, it diminished the seriousness of getting up to dance in the living room.

Cole held her loosely and looked down at her with a grin while their shoes stuck to the carpet. "Not exactly the best dance floor, is it?"

"I feel a little foolish," Charlie confessed.

"Haven't you ever danced in the middle of the day before?"

"Frankly, no. Have you?"

Cole sighed dramatically. "Sweetheart, there's little I haven't tried." His lips curved into a teasing smile. "But I've never danced with a gorgeous blonde on pale blue carpeting before."

He was flirting, acting very, very differently than she'd expected. Why? To make her feel at ease? If that was it, it was working. The apprehension she'd arrived with was gone; she was having fun. And this was a side of Cole she hadn't even suspected. He was a multifaceted individual, a charmer when he wanted to be, a hard businessman, also when he wanted to be.

Couldn't she be the same?

Yes, why not? She found him unutterably appealing on a personal level. It was in business where antagonism arose. But maybe even that would be eliminated, should some dear soul pop up with a piece of timberland he would trade for an excellent fishing stream.

Without business pressures she could "like" Cole without reservations, couldn't she? And even put the past behind her?

The mood of their dancing was altering. Cole wasn't smiling so openly now. His eyes looked a deeper blue and she could see a strong pulse beat in his temple. He wet his lips. "Charlie . . . ?"

"Yes?"

Cole dropped her hand and locked his arms around her waist. "This is how I wanted to hold you at the Buckhorn," he said softly, bringing her up against himself.

She gave a small laugh and dared to slide her hands up to his shoulders. A delightful tingle had begun within her, intensifying as she looked up into his eyes. Her voice had grown husky. "We didn't exactly dance like enemies that night, Cole. I'm sure the gossips have had a field day since the Fourth."

"Does gossip bother you?"

Charlie smiled faintly. "To a degree, I suppose. Doesn't it bother you?"

"Only if it's a lie. If people get a kick out of telling each other that you and I danced together and obviously enjoyed it, let 'em talk."

"And that we left together," she reminded.

"Yes, and we left together." He laughed quietly. "I suppose they could make a lot out of that, all right. They probably wouldn't want to believe all we did was exchange a few kisses, would they?"

Charlie shrugged. "Who knows? I think the local gossip is pretty harmless most of the time."

Cole raised an eyebrow. "What do you think they're saying—that you and I are having an affair?"

"Could be," she murmured, recognizing the sensual turn of topic and tone of voice.

"Then we've got the name without the game." Cole stopped stock-still, and his hands came up to her face. His eyes radiated a new tension as he stared down at her. "Do you know how beautiful you are?"

She tried to laugh, but it was a poor effort. Her insides were churning too much for levity. She knew he was going to kiss her, and probably not stop at one or two kisses, either. Now was the time to object, if she was going to. They were at a very obvious fork in the road, and he wasn't pushing. It was up to her.

Their eyes met, and she was hit with such a thundering desire she couldn't even speak. His handsome face drew nearer, then his lips grazed hers. "You have such a kissable mouth," he whispered. "It's haunted my dreams since your first visit here."

Charlie's eyelashes fluttered downward as her gaze lingered on his mouth. She could easily say the same thing to him. Many, many times her wayward thoughts had been on his sexy mouth.

Sex. That's what this was all about. Cole reached the woman in her easier than anyone else ever had. With little or no apparent effort he kept her alert to her own femininity, something she sometimes lost track of in her absorption with screeching sawmill equipment, production schedules, quality control and that accursed lack of timber.

But sex was a part of living, an instinctive need like hunger and thirst. It wasn't sex with Cole she'd been fighting,

Charlie suddenly realized. From the first, he'd made her think of making love. It was everything else Cole represented that caused her such misery.

Couldn't she forget that, at least for today? They liked each other, they wanted each other. They weren't children, they were hurting no one. And if they made love once and never again, well, maybe it was time she experienced a one-night stand, even if this was a Sunday afternoon.

His lips came down again, this time firmly, and his arms dropped around her. Clasping her hands behind his neck, Charlie closed her eyes as they rocked to the slow beat of the music. Their feet never moved, and the kiss was long and sweetly undemanding.

Waves of delicious languor washed away another layer of her inhibitions. Nothing this wonderful could be wrong. This big, powerful man felt like heaven on earth, and with each passing moment she allowed a deeper commitment.

This was how he wanted her, Cole thought exultantly, with space, with time. He'd been right to stop Friday night. The bittersweet hours since then had only added to the pleasure they would have now, and his arms tightened around her and his blood surged with increased desire.

She was soft against him, molding to his body, a union imperfect only because of their clothing. They kissed again and again, unhurriedly, sensually, their lips mating and retreating in complete harmony.

Then he looked at her, and the haze of passion he saw in her green eyes brought an explosive need. He was aroused almost to the point of pain within his suddenly too tight jeans, and he wanted to shed all barriers and have her splendidly naked.

And oddly, surprisingly intermingled with his intense desire was a tenderness—that special feeling he'd been trying to understand. Words escaped him for the moment and Charlie said nothing, either, but the look they exchanged spoke volumes. He saw a yes in her eyes and drew her head to his chest. "You know I care for you, don't you?" he murmured huskily.

The words warmed her; maybe they were what she had wanted to hear. He hadn't said "love," which she wouldn't have believed, perhaps thinking it a line, a contrivance for seduction. But "caring" was acceptable, appropriate for the sexuality in the air. She could even admit the same without giving up anything, and she was about to until Cole's mouth took hers again.

This was a hungry kiss and it ripped everything from her mind but the searing emotion between them. His hands were no longer content to rest behind her. They roamed, up and down her back, cupping her derriere, bringing her closer, closer. His bulging manhood was a physical reminder of his fervor, pressing into her abdomen, too far from the ache in her body, and she rose to her toes to feel the proof of his need more intimately.

She felt her skirt being drawn up, then his hands beneath it pushing into her underpants. His palms held the curves of her hips and stroked her bare skin. They'd gone this far... and she had chosen to let it happen.

Cole's eyes glazed with desire. He stepped back and swept her up into his arms, heading for his bedroom and his bed, which was big and soft.

He wasn't some sex-starved kid, and he planned to savor every moment with this special woman. But still, his mind leaped ahead to what the day had time for. They could make love for hours, they could take a whirlpool bath together, they could have dinner and make love again ... and again. That's how much he wanted her. Not just once, but again and again.

How did he know that when they'd done so little yet? It puzzled him, but it wasn't a question to dig into now. They were at last on his bed, stretched out, and their kisses were no longer lasting and tender. They were gasping, needful, urgent. He pushed the straps of her sundress from her shoulders and kissed the soft skin he uncovered. He undid buttons and felt her hands beneath his shirt, as eager as his.

He sat up, pulled the shirt over his head and returned to the delightful task of undressing her, thrilled with Charlie's pleasure in his naked torso. His broad chest was matted with dark hair, his skin taut and smooth, and while he opened her dress and groaned at the sight of her beautiful breasts, she took equal delight in the perfection of his masculinity.

It was a moment of almost unbearable tension when they were both finally naked, for they wanted to see and touch at the same time. "You're gorgeous . . . incredible," Cole whispered, running his hands up and down her body.

"So are you," she returned hoarsely.

He gathered her into a smothering embrace, joining their bare bodies from shoulders to thighs. At the very center of the embrace, the core of all their pleasure and torment, the hard length of his manhood pressed into her, and Charlie's thoughts were concentrated on it. Had she ever been so obsessed with a man's body before?

His mouth teased hers, nipping gently, tugging at her bottom lip. Then he began kissing a downward trail, lingering at her throat, stopping for long, delicious minutes at her breasts. His tongue was a feverish lover, arousing her nipples to firmness, drugging her senses with rapture, and she gasped aloud when his hand found her most sensitive spot.

Her head moved back and forth on the pillow in the purest ecstasy of her life. He wasn't just a man any longer, he was the most important man in the world. He was pleasure and need and excitement and everything sensuous rolled up into one beautiful, soul-searing package, and any doubts she'd had about the wisdom of a personal involvement with him were so much dust. How could she, or any other woman, deny herself a man like Cole?

"Sweetheart, your braid," Cole murmured, rising to a sitting position and drawing her up with him. "I want to undo it."

His touch was gentle and soon her flaxen mane was brushing her shoulders. Cole twined his fingers in it and brought it around her face, his eyes a dark, intense blue while he stared. "This is the way I want it," he whispered. "Charlie, you've bewitched me."

Her smile was weak, almost a question. "Maybe we've bewitched each other."

"Lie back. I want to see your hair on the pillow." Cole threw one sinewy thigh over hers as she sank back down, and he leaned over her. Tenderly his fingers traced her features. "Do you feel bewitched, too?"

She swallowed. "I feel . . . Cole, I . . ."

"I know, sweetheart. You feel what I do. I want you like I've never wanted anything before." His hand traveled a slow circling downward path again. "Kiss me," he whispered.

Her lips separated and the tip of her tongue slowly circled them. Cole froze as he watched the sensual ritual, then brought his head down. Their gazes locked in silent communion while he repeated what she'd just done—trace the outline of her mouth with the tip of his tongue. "Cole . . ." she whispered throatily.

"It's delicious torture, isn't it?"

"Yes," she whispered.

Her lips were swollen from kisses, but she pressed the back of his head down for more, taking his mouth and tongue with a groan. She arched her body, lifting her hips to his caressing hand, and fell back to the bed when it was where she needed it. His touch was tender but purposeful, creating more delicious torture. His mouth left hers to capture a breast again, and she closed her eyes as desire built to a fever pitch.

Then he was gone. Her eyes flashed open. "Cole . . . ?"

His voice was soothing. "I'm just being careful, sweetheart."

"Oh, yes, of course," she whispered, grateful that he'd thought of protection.

In a moment he was back, warm, solid, drawing her close again. Their lips touched, and she felt his move with words. "Tell me you want me."

Her head bobbed. "I do. I want you very much. You can tell, can't you?"

His voice was ragged. "Yes, but I wanted to hear it. Do you want me now, sweetheart?"

She was nearly delirious with bursting passion. "Now," she whimpered huskily.

He raised himself over her, and his entry into her aching, desirous body brought a cry of exquisite pleasure from her lips. At once Charlie was lost on a vast, wild sea. Cole pushed his hands beneath her hips and lifted her pelvis to his deep, rhythmic thrusts. His breathing was loud in her ear, for his head rested on the pillow beside hers, and the wondrous chafing of his strokes lifted her higher and higher into something she magically found the strength to marvel at.

"Charlie . . . Charlie," she heard in her ear, rasped in gravelly tones. "You're perfect . . . perfect. Small . . . hot . . . I'll never get enough of you . . . never."

Drowning in such words, inundated with a wild, mindless passion, she matched Cole's rhythm, feeling every movement, every breath, every heartbeat between them as one. Her world expanded, encompassed the moon and the stars, and when scorching waves of pleasure hit her, she cried out and dug her nails into Cole's back. In moments his voice echoed her joy, and he drew the final ecstasy out to the fullest with a flurry of heated movements.

Then the room was silent, except for the sound of their breathing. Cole weighted her down, their bodies damp with perspiration.

Reality was a long time in returning...and Charlie made no effort to hurry it.

9

COLE COOKED THE STEAKS on the outside grill and Charlie made the salad. Then, along with a good cabernet, they sat down to eat in the dining room. The sun was beginning to weaken in the western sky and Cole brought candlesticks to the table, adding a romantic touch to the meal.

Both of them were in robes. Charlie was wearing one of white terry that Cole said his sister or one of his sisters-in-law had left behind, and Cole was in navy-blue velour.

They were having fun, laughing and talking easily, sipping wine, enjoying a camaraderie that amazed Charlie. Cole was good company, even beyond the thrill she got every time she stopped to realize what the day had evolved into.

Scrupulously she avoided mentioning business, and several times when Cole veered in that direction, Charlie skillfully changed the subject. As long as they steered clear of that, she was comfortable with him. But there were still too many hurts connected with business to risk a discussion.

The distant past was a safe topic, and they exchanged dozens of childhood and growing-up stories, laughing over some, commiserating over others. They both had lost beloved parents, both grown up around sawmills, Cole in Oregon, Charlie in Montana. They had a lot of common background and they sat at the table long after their plates were empty, just talking.

When the bottle of wine was drained, Charlie stood up. "I'll help you clean up, then I probably should be going."

Cole pulled her down on his lap with a laugh. "Not so fast." He wrapped his arms around her, breathing in her scent. "Today has been so great, Charlie."

"Yes," she readily agreed.

He tilted his head back to see her face. "You were worried when you got here, weren't you?"

"Very."

"But you're not worried now?"

She hesitated. "There are still . . ."

The day had been so perfect, he'd hoped any doubts she'd arrived with had disappeared. But they were still behind her eyes, vaguer maybe, but there. "Don't say it," he pleaded, bringing her head down so their lips could meet. His kiss was warm, and Charlie wound her arms around his neck and kissed him back. When he slid a hand under her robe, she had no objection. His touch was wonderful, arousing, and she knew that any feelings she'd had for Cole before they'd made love had magnified a hundred times.

"You don't have to hurry off, do you?" he whispered against her lips. His hand was between her thighs, once again lighting fires that had been so satisfactorily banked earlier, or so Charlie had thought.

"What have you got in mind?" she teased softly.

"What do you think?"

They had made love twice before dinner, and now the excitement was growing again. It was truly the most thrilling day Charlie had ever spent with a man, and it obviously wasn't over yet.

"How about a whirlpool bath together?" Cole asked, nuzzling the robe apart at her breasts and taking one lush nipple into his mouth. He sucked gently and Charlie's eyelids drifted shut with pure delight.

"A whirlpool bath?" she murmured huskily. "I've never taken a bath with anyone before."

"Then you're in for a treat, sweetheart. Come on." Cole brought them both to their feet and they started from the dining room, arm in arm.

It had grown dark while they sat at the table and the headlights of a vehicle ascending the bluff suddenly intruded into the candlelit room. "Hell," Cole muttered. "Who can that be?"

Charlie's heart thudded. Cole's house was so far off the beaten path that it hadn't occurred to her someone might just drop in. Her pickup was parked right outside, and everyone in the county knew what her old truck looked like. And here she was, in a robe!

"I'm going to get dressed," she cried, and she dashed down the hall, her heart palpitating anxiously.

But she wanted to hear how Cole handled the visitor, and once out of sight Charlie stopped and listened. She nearly fainted when she heard Rick Slaughter's voice.

Cole wasn't exactly cordial. "What the hell are you doing out here, Rick?"

Charlie could picture the scene even if she couldn't see it—Cole in a robe, her pickup outside—and her mouth got so dry she could hardly swallow. Then, Rick asking "Isn't that Charlie McAllister's truck?" undid her for sure.

"Yeah," Cole responded brusquely. "So what?"

"Hell, doesn't mean anything to me, Cole," Rick answered.

"Like hell it doesn't," Charlie mumbled, knowing it would be all over the county tomorrow.

"What I came by for," Rick went on, "was to tell you that Jess Lathrop's got a problem with . . ."

Charlie knew Jess was one of Canfield's biggest loggers, and she had no desire to hear about his problems. Leaving her hiding place, she hurried to Cole's bedroom, cussing under her breath every step of the way.

She found her dress and looked for her underpants, frowning while she threw rumpled sheets aside. Cole came in and saw what she was doing. "What are you looking for?"

She glared at him. "For my underwear, dammit!" Charlie bent over and peered under the bed.

"Hey, don't let this throw you," Cole cautioned, advancing into the room.

"Don't let it throw me!" She rolled her eyes in exasperation. "Of all the people to come along!"

Cole put his hands on her shoulders. "Are you ashamed of being here?"

"No, I'm not ashamed. It's no one else's business, but dammit, Cole, everyone will be talking about it now." Her head dropped and she put her forehead against his chest.

He stroked her hair. "If you're not ashamed, honey, let 'em talk."

Her voice was muffled. "But why Rick? He's the worst person that could have come along."

"Why?" Cole took her chin and raised her face. "Why is Rick the worst?"

Charlie felt positively miserable. "Because I can't stand him, that's why. And because he . . ."

"He what?" Cole insisted.

Charlie shrugged out of his grasp. "He's asked me out several times, and I know he's spiteful because I said no."

Cole's face looked suddenly tense. "You don't think that has anything to do with the timber sales, do you?"

"Why. . .no. That never occurred to me. In fact, it's impossible. No, I don't think that at all. He outbid Pete and the others as well as me, you know."

There, it was said again, and instantly the old tension of the subject was in the room with them. Charlie drew a dejected breath. "I think I better go, Cole."

"I don't want this ruining things between us."

Her chin came up. "We'll try not to let it."

A spark of anger entered Cole's eyes. "It already is! And you're letting it happen. Why, for God's sake?"

Charlie started going through the bedclothes again. "I'm not *letting* anything happen. There are other things to consider besides what happened here today." Triumphantly she spotted a bit of white and grabbed her underpants.

She saw the glower, the indecision on his face, the anger he was trying to hold back, and she softened. "Cole, this was a wonderful day, but the real world still goes on. Tomorrow means I slip back into my slot and you slip back into yours. I knew that when I came here. Rick showing up just made it happen sooner than it should have, that's all."

"I won't listen to such hogwash," Cole said with a snort. "Today was real, maybe the most real thing that's ever happened to me. And if it doesn't mean the same to you, then you're right to go off in a huff."

"I'm not in a huff!" she cried.

"What would you call it? Fifteen minutes ago we were aching to make love again." Cole rushed forward and grabbed her arms. "Charlie, you're clinging to old hurts that will never do anything but cause new ones. Can't you forget all that foolishness? We've got something . . ."

"It's not foolishness," she snapped. "That's something you and I will never see eye to eye on. Even if our present situation turned around and I was out from under that miserable contract, we wouldn't agree on what really happened the past two years."

"Miserable contract! Is that how you still look at our agreement?"

This was getting out of hand. They were shouting and Cole's fingers were digging into her arms. Cole wasn't one to back down from a fight, and neither was she. It could only go from bad to worse, and they still wouldn't agree.

Charlie tore her arms free and headed for the bathroom. "I'll get dressed and leave," she announced stiffly.

She came out a few minutes later to a vacant room, but the robe Cole had been wearing was thrown across the foot of the bed. She tossed the white one next to it and left the bedroom.

Cole was in the kitchen, wearing his jeans and shirt, leaning against the counter waiting for her. "I didn't see Rick pay any particular attention to you last Friday night at the Buckhorn," he said coolly.

"You're right," Charlie replied tartly. "Maybe he's given up on me, which, by the way, would be the luckiest break I've had in a long time." Remembering she'd left her purse in the living room, she started away.

Cole followed. "You're dead wrong about a lot of things, Charlie, and too stubborn to admit it. No one did anything wrong on those timber sales and you know it. As far as Rick chasing you, well, you have a right not to like the guy personally, but . . ."

She spun around. "Well, thank you for your permission, which I don't need! Would you like to know what I really think of Rick Slaughter? I wouldn't be one bit surprised if *he* started that fire."

At Cole's stunned expression the anger drained from Charlie. My God, where had that ghastly accusation come from? She hadn't thought of it before, not once. But Cole had made her so darned mad it was a wonder she hadn't accused him of setting the fire!

"I . . . I didn't mean that," she mumbled. "Cole, I've got to leave. I'm saying things I don't even mean."

He watched her silently, his eyes dark and turbulent. What was the basis for the antagonism between Charlie and Rick? What had really gone on the two years he hadn't been around much? A distant dread curled in his mind, mingling with speculation on the fire.

Charlie was leaving . . . she was nearly to the front door.

Damn, she had him as crazy as she was acting. Suspecting Rick was ridiculous! "Charlie, wait a minute!" Cole ran to intercept her.

She stopped and turned. "I've got to go, Cole," she said sadly, terribly shaken over the last half hour, maybe shaken over the whole day now that it might become public knowledge.

"I know. I'm not trying to stop you. But it can't end here. When can we see each other again? Tomorrow night for dinner?" Cole asked, rubbing the back of his neck. "No, I can't tomorrow night," he corrected, "I've got a dinner meeting. Tuesday evening?"

Charlie released an emotional breath. "I don't know, Cole. Let's give this some time, all right?"

He felt his body tensing again. "I'll call you Tuesday."

She nodded. "Yes, do that. Good night."

THE NEXT MORNING, with the mill running at top speed and Joan at the front desk, Charlie went into her office and closed the door. She settled down with the local phone book and proceeded to call the realtors in the area, informing each of them of her desire to make a property trade. A few of them expressed interest, but one, Roger Cook of Three Forks Realty, became excited. "I've already got some folks in mind, Charlie. I'll contact them and get back to you."

"Wonderful. I'll be waiting for your call, Roger." Charlie's nerves were standing right on edge this morning. During several bouts of sleeplessness last night she'd come to the conclusion that if she didn't get out of that contract, she and Cole didn't stand a chance.

And she needed to be given a chance so badly that she was afraid to hope she'd get it. Her feelings for Cole kept multiplying, and just thinking of him made her knees weak. But she couldn't contemplate any sort of future together unless she was independent again.

Did that make sense?

She asked herself that question a dozen times, adding another each time: why couldn't she leave things alone and be happy working for him?

But that was like trying to figure out why she preferred chicken over fish, or liked certain colors better than others. It was just the way she was—unable to give her heart to a man she felt less than equal to.

All day the conversation with Roger Cook lay in her stomach like a dead weight, keeping her tense and anxious. Around three, on her way back from the mill, Charlie saw a red Canfield pickup pulling in. Cole! She hurried her steps, thrilled that he'd come by in spite of her desultory parting remarks last night.

But it wasn't Cole who got out of the truck; it was Rick Slaughter!

Deflated, disappointed and immediately on guard, Charlie proceeded at a slower pace. What did he want, a chance to gloat? To make some smart remark about where she'd been last night?

Rick saw her coming and leaned against the pickup with his arms folded. He wore a big cowboy hat and his face was shadowed, but Charlie could see the smugness in his stance. God, he was annoying.

"Hello, Charlie," he drawled.

"Rick," she acknowledged coolly.

"Just passing by," he announced, "and thought I'd stop and say hello. Haven't seen much of you lately, what with no timber sales for a while."

Since when did he feel chummy enough to stop for a hello? It was on the tip of Charlie's tongue to ask him, but she managed to bite it back. "What do you want, Rick?"

He stood away from the truck. "Do I have to want something?"

"In that case, you'll have to excuse me. I have work to do." Charlie started away.

"Charlie!"

She turned, unable to conceal her impatience. "What?"

"I just want to give you some advice."

Flabbergasted at his gall, Charlie snorted. "*You* want to give *me* advice?"

"Yeah. It's pretty clear what you're up to. Cole told me what you said about me."

"I beg your pardon!" Charlie cut in. Rick didn't look whiny and oily now; he looked mean. But while it registered, Charlie was too upset to let it deter her growing anger. "What I'm up to is none of your business."

"That's where you're wrong. I hear you had a little fire here one night."

Charlie's heart nearly stopped. My Lord, had her wild accusation hit closer to the mark than she'd thought? There was something threatening in Rick's voice, a note that sent a chill up her spine. "Everyone's heard I had a fire," she retorted bravely. "It's old news, Rick."

He glanced off toward the mill building. "Sure would have been a shame if that fire had gotten out of control," he remarked coyly.

Her eyes narrowed. "Are you threatening me?"

Innocence instantly spread across his face. "Now why would I do that? You're too suspicious, Charlie. But I've always said you were a smart cookie. I'm sure you get the picture. Just be careful what you say to my boss. Pillow talk sometimes gets out of hand." With a self-satisfied grin Rick climbed into his pickup. "So long, babe," he called insolently.

Frozen to the spot, Charlie watched him drive away. Rick *had* threatened her. She'd never thought him dangerous, but she was fast revising that opinion. My Lord, was this enough to bring to the sheriff? Rick would lie out of it, of course, and it would come down to her word against his. What should she do?

Cole came to mind, and with this thought another question arose: should she tell him what Rick had just said?

Weakly Charlie acknowledged that after her angry accusation last night, Cole probably wouldn't believe her. They were still on shaky ground where Rick was concerned, first-class snake that he was. He had Cole conned, and he liked his situation enough to threaten someone who might be in a position to influence his boss. Was he up to more than outbidding everyone on government timber sales?

Suspicions ran rampant in Charlie's mind, about the fire, about what else Rick might have been involved in. She had nothing concrete, but she *knew* he'd started the second fire, and it made her ill to realize there was nothing she could do about it.

ROGER COOK DIDN'T CALL until nine that evening. Charlie was getting ready for bed, exhausted from little sleep the night before and the extremely trying day she'd just had.

"Sorry to call you at home, Charlie, but I just now got hold of my clients. I'll come right to the point: they're interested."

For the first time today Charlie breathed freely.

"If you've got a minute, I'll tell you about the property they've got to trade."

"Please do," she begged, and settled down to hear about the Copley property—two hundred acres whose wealthy, absentee owners were much more interested in a good fishing stream than the value of the timber on their land.

"And they understand I can only trade, Roger?"

"They understand perfectly. They'll be out here this coming weekend. In the meantime, I thought you might want to take a look at their land. What do you think?"

Charlie smiled. "I think yes."

"I'll come by the mill tomorrow afternoon and pick you up."

That night Charlie slept wonderfully well, and she even allowed a few fantasies before she closed her eyes, fantasies in which Cole had the starring role.

THE MILL HAD a serious breakdown just before noon the next day. Charlie spent two hours with the millwright finding the source of the electrical problem, then walked back into the office sweaty and grimy, planning to wash up before Roger Cook arrived. Joan greeted her with a handful of phone messages and said, "Cole Morgan called twice, Charlie."

Just his name caused a physical reaction and a flash of memory that magically included hours of incredible lovemaking. "Thanks, Joan," she murmured, intending to return Cole's calls the minute she was ready for Roger.

But when she came out of the bathroom, reasonably clean and put together again, Roger was walking in. Charlie glanced at her office longingly and contemplated asking Roger to wait, but she decided against it and offered her hand to the realtor. "I really appreciate this, Roger," she said, shaking his hand firmly.

"I'll be well paid by my clients, Charlie. If that stream is anywhere near like you say it is and you like the Copley's property, I'm pretty sure you've got a deal."

"Dad always claimed it was better than the Blue Ribbon fishing around the state, Roger."

"If your dad said it, then it's true. Ready to go?"

The realtor was anxious to get started, but halfway to the door Charlie stopped and turned to Joan. "If Cole calls again, tell him..." She hesitated, uncertain what to tell Cole. She'd rather he didn't know about the possible trade yet, she realized. "Just tell him I had to leave on business and I'll be home this evening," she finally instructed.

IT WAS AFTER DARK before Charlie got back. Roger dropped her at the mill to get her pickup and she drove the three miles home, tired, dirty and so pleased with the day that she could think of nothing else.

The land Roger had shown her was crowded with timber, and if there was any problem at all with it, it was that at least half of the trees were too large for her mill to handle. That meant one of two things: either she paid a logger a high price to log selectively or she sold the large timber to Canfield. That the shoe was possibly on the other foot now, should she and the Copleys strike a deal, was almost laughable. Instead of cutting Canfield's small logs, Cole might end up cutting her large timber.

The mere thought of broaching the subject with Cole gave Charlie a shiver, however, and she took refuge in the fact that she didn't have to do anything right now. The ball was presently in the Copleys' court; she had to wait for their inspection of her property and decision. Then, if the trade went through, she would talk to Cole about it.

When she turned into her driveway and saw the black Lincoln, she got weak. It hadn't occurred to her Cole might be there, and why should it? She couldn't possibly have pictured Cole Morgan having the patience, or even the desire, to wait at her house for her, even if she hadn't returned his calls.

But he was there all right, on the porch swing, and as she crossed the lawn he stood up. "You've put in quite a day," he said quietly.

"Hello, Cole," she replied, taking the stairs warily.

"Anything wrong? Joan said you'd be home this evening."

"Yes, I planned to be." Charlie sensed his hope of an explanation, but she couldn't talk about it yet. After the weekend, after the Copleys inspected her land and decided, then she would tell Cole.

But she could apologize. "I'm sorry I'm so late," she said, unlocking the front door and switching on the hall light. "Would you like to come in?"

"I didn't wait out here for two hours just to say hi," he replied a tad sarcastically.

"No, of course you didn't."

Cole's clean crispness magnified her soiled clothing and disarray. "Would you mind if I took a quick shower?"

His eyes moved over her, then one corner of his mouth turned up. "Want me to wash your back?"

It took Charlie by surprise, but also brought an instantaneous flash of warm relief. He wasn't angry over the unreturned calls and long wait, and with that lovely little half smile on his face, even Sunday night's confrontation seemed less menacing to the new relationship they'd begun that day. Still . . . was he serious about washing her back?

Charlie's eyes blazed with the thought, and Cole laughed. "Go on, take your shower. Maybe I'll just help dry you off."

She relaxed into laughter. "I'll put some coffee on first. Have you had dinner?"

"Haven't you?" Cole followed her into the kitchen.

"No. But I'll fix a sandwich later." Charlie rinsed the pot and filled it with fresh water, aware that Cole was watching her closely. He was still curious over what she'd been doing all day, she sensed. "I meant to call you back," she said apologetically.

"But you didn't." Cole leaned a shoulder against the refrigerator door. "I was afraid you weren't going to."

Her gaze moved to him. "I was going to," she stated quietly. She saw questions in his wonderful blue eyes and avoided them again by turning back to the coffeepot. When it was ready and switched on, she smiled and started for the door. "I'll just be a minute."

She didn't get past Cole. He caught her and pulled her into his arms. "Charlie . . ." he whispered, his lips in her hair.

"I'm dirty," she protested weakly.

"You're beautiful. Do you have any idea what long legs in tight jeans do to me?"

"These long legs need a bath," she said, sighing. He had so much power over her senses, enough to knock down her defenses with a touch.

"Give me a kiss, then I'll let you go."

It was said lightly, almost teasingly, and Charlie smiled and raised her chin. "All right, kiss away."

It started out easy, just a sweet pressure that sent darting thrills through Charlie. But it changed swiftly, evolving into a storm of craving that left them both breathless. "God, what you do to me," Cole whispered when they came up for air. His eyes were dark pools. "Maybe I should wash your back."

"I'll opt for the drying off, if you don't object."

Cole drew an unsteady breath. "You've got it, sweetheart. Can I wait in your bedroom?"

"You can wait anyplace your little heart desires." She laughed, rising to give him another kiss, this one a brief, happy kiss.

That happiness wasn't fake, Charlie decided as they climbed the stairs. Cole did make her happy, happy in a way no one ever had before. She led the way into her bedroom and swept her hand out in a grand gesture. "Here you have it, my boudoir, sir. Make yourself comfortable while I get rid of the sweat of my hard labor."

Cole plopped full length on the bed. "Is this comfortable enough?"

Laughing, Charlie left the room. While she peeled her dirty clothes away in the bathroom she realized she wasn't tired anymore. The thought of Cole in her house, in her bed, was so exciting she was light-headed.

And there wasn't anybody to come around and disrupt and embarrass them, either, as Rick Slaughter had done.

Charlie turned the water on with a frown at the thought of Rick. He had started that fire and he had threatened her. She should march back to the bedroom and tell Cole what kind of jerk his timber supervisor really was. But it would only cause another argument, wouldn't it? There was more to Rick's threats, too, something she couldn't put a finger on but kept going through her mind in waves of suspicion.

Why was he so worried about her and Cole? That's what it boiled down to—how influential she might be with Cole. It was odd, very odd. And foolish on Rick's part. For every time his name came up, Cole jumped to his defense. Rick was a sore subject between her and Cole, impossible to discuss without anger.

After the weekend things could change drastically, Charlie realized again. And how welcome it would be to be totally independent and in a position to put Rick and the past away for good. In the meantime she would thank her lucky stars that the way Sunday had ended up hadn't damaged what she and Cole had begun earlier.

Fifteen minutes later Charlie slipped on the robe that was always hanging on a hook on the bathroom door and crossed the hall.

Cole's clothes were on a chair, and Charlie looked from them to the bed. He was under a carelessly draped end of the sheet and waiting for her, and there was no mistaking the lustful gleam in his eyes. "You dried yourself," he accused softly.

Charlie stepped to the edge of the bed. "I had to dry my hair."

"I love it. Come here." He drew the sheet back in invitation, boldly displaying his very ready charms to her gaze. "Come here and let me love you."

The sensual words melted her into a soft, liquid smile. Slowly, provocatively, she untied the sash of the robe and let it slide down her body to the floor. Cole looked at her as though it were the first time and held up his arms. "Come here, sweetheart," he whispered.

She sat on the bed, placed a hand on his chest and leaned down to kiss him. Her hair draped around them while her lips moved on his, and she felt him clasp the back of her head. She slipped her tongue into his mouth and heard a small growl in his throat. Her breasts swayed against his chest, a delicious friction that hardened her nipples and created ripples of pleasure in both her and Cole.

She raised her head and looked at him. "You're a very sexy man," she whispered, leaning across him and stroking the thick, dark hair from his forehead. A female satisfaction noted the glaze of desire in his eyes.

"You're teasing me," Cole said with a funny, surprised expression.

She smiled mysteriously and let her fingertips drift down to his mouth, where she evaded his attempts to capture them with his lips. "Let me make love to you," she whispered, and saw twin flames ignite in his eyes.

His nod was slow and sensuous and he dropped his hands to the bed. Charlie's pulse was running wild, and she took a calming breath and let her eyes begin at his and then make a slow, downward study. She felt his reaction to being so visually examined in the tensing of his body, but she took her time and admired the strong lines of his chest and tight belly.

The sheet bulged at his lap, and languorously she slid it down, hearing Cole's breath catch in a sound that made her heart skip a beat. For a long, erotic moment she just looked at his magnificent maleness, then at his hard, beautiful thighs. She moistened her suddenly dry lips with a flick of her tongue.

"Are you trying to drive me crazy?" Cole rasped thickly.

Her eyes swept up to his. "Is that what I'm doing?"

"Very close."

"Didn't you do something like this to me Sunday?" she purred.

"Did it drive you crazy?"

"Very close."

Their eyes met, then Charlie smiled and stretched out beside him, but on her side so she could look down on him. Supporting herself on an elbow, she began tracing little patterns on his chest. "I like touching you," she whispered. "Do you like me touching you?"

"You know I do," Cole growled.

She dipped her head and licked at a nipple. "Do you like that, too?"

"Charlie . . ." he groaned.

She trailed kisses across his chest, then pressed her lips just beneath his jaw. "You smell spicy," she murmured.

"After-shave," he muttered.

"I like it." Moving up, her lips circled his mouth. She felt his hands lift from the bed and come around her, and he moved his head to find her mouth. He was greedy, hungry, and he pulled her on top of him, kissing her hard while he settled her between his thighs.

Flushed and breathing irregularly, she raised her head to see him. "Who's in command here?" she gasped.

His eyes were dark with passion. "I want you."

Maintaining eye contact, she adjusted her position and slid downward, taking him inside of her velvety warmth. "Like this?" she whispered.

His hands moved to her hair and twisted within it. "Exactly like that," he echoed hoarsely.

Anchoring her knees on each side of his hips, she slowly sat up. "Maybe like this?"

He closed his eyes and let go of a powerful breath. "Yeah, that's perfect."

She lifted and slid back and watched the pleasure on his face, her own pleasure reaching her very soul. Feelings swirled within her, so many feelings, some touching on the familiar, some so alien she was afraid to analyze them. She could love this man so easily, she knew, if there weren't so many outside influences in the relationship.

Someday...someday when things were different... And they would be different . . . maybe very soon. . . .

"Charlie . . . sweetheart . . ." Cole rasped, taking hold of her hips for deeper thrusts. She rode him with steady, sure strokes, closing her eyes at the mounting tension, unable to stop the sweeping hot waves threatening her control. She hadn't expected them so soon, and she fell forward with a soft cry. His hands clasped around her and he held her until she quieted.

Her voice was shaky when she raised her head. "I'm sorry."

"Sorry! What for? You gave me a beautiful gift, Charlie." He brought her to the bed and leaned over her, touching her face with gentle fingertips. "What just happened is special to me, Charlie."

"You affect me so strongly," she whispered.

"You do the same to me." He kissed her lips then smiled at her. "It's best we stopped when we did, anyway. I got so involved I forgot about protection." His eyes held hers. "That wouldn't be too good, would it? You wouldn't want a baby, would you?"

There was something so intense in his eyes, she looked away from it. How should she answer? A baby? Cole's baby? Her heart fluttered, then calmed. She brought her eyes back to his. "It wouldn't be very wise, would it?" she responded thinly.

He studied her, then smiled. "No, not very wise."

10

AFTER A BITE of peanut butter sandwich, Charlie washed it down with a gulp of cold milk. Cole laughed and asked, "Is that any kind of meal for a growing girl?"

"I stopped growing many years ago, my love," she quipped.

"Am I?"

"Are you what?"

"Your love?"

They were sitting cross-legged on the bed, Charlie back in the robe, Cole with a sheet over his lap. His question caught her unprepared and she dropped her eyes to the sandwich. "Do you want to be?" she asked softly.

"Do you want me to be?"

Her gaze lifted and they studied each other. The air was heavy suddenly, full of electricity. They had just made wonderful love, moving, passionate, satisfying love, and yet they were reluctant to speak their feelings. They were like children in a way, each daring the other to "go first."

Charlie sighed, understanding her own reluctance, questioning Cole's. Yet his was understandable, too. With her so cautious, could she fault a hesitancy on his part to expose a possible vulnerability?

Only time could take care of their conflict, and time would if her plans gelled. Once everything was right in her world again she could look Cole in the eye and say, "I'm falling in love with you." But not yet, not tonight, no matter how moving their lovemaking had been.

Cole stretched out again, one arm crooked beneath his head, with a sigh that equalled Charlie's in frustration. "I wonder if we'll ever be able to be totally open with one another," he mused.

Reaching across him, Charlie put her plate and glass on the bed stand. Her breasts brushed his arm and he gave her a raised-eyebrow look. "If you do that, how can we have a serious conversation?"

"Do what? All I did was . . ."

A wicked gleam entered Cole's vivid blue eyes, and he lunged up suddenly and brought her to the bed. On her back, staring up at him, Charlie grinned. "A woman isn't safe around you, you sex fiend."

"Pushing your pillows into a man isn't exactly behaving like a woman who doesn't want to arouse a sex fiend, sweetheart."

"My pillows!" Charlie hooted with laughter.

"Let's take a look at those gorgeous pillows," Cole teased, untying the robe's sash. He spread the silky fabric, and then he wasn't teasing anymore. His eyes devoured her femaleness and his hands trembled as he caressed the soft flesh. "You really are a beautiful woman," he whispered.

Charlie caught her lower lip between her teeth. Watching his handsome face while he enjoyed her body was arousing in itself, an eroticism only Cole had taught her. He had taught her so many things, like how a fingernail trailing up his spine caused a sensual shudder in his body, a dozen other intimacies that only lovers could know about each other.

Despite each of them holding something back, they were close, Charlie realized, close in a way she would never get over should things not work out for them. Looking back, her life didn't seem very meaningful before Cole came into it. If he should suddenly be out of it . . .

A shiver raised goose bumps on her skin, a reaction Charlie wasn't sure had been caused by Cole's hands or her own thoughts.

"Do you have some lotion handy?" he asked with a rakish grin.

"Lotion? What for?"

"I want to put it on you."

Her breath caught.

"Don't look so shocked," he said, laughing.

"I'm not shocked," she denied, but she was—shocked in a way that thrilled her beyond words. "There's some in the bathroom."

"I'll get it." Cole was gone and back in seconds, walking around naked as a jaybird and not the least bit put off by it. He kneeled on the bed. "Slip your robe off, sweetheart. This will either put you to sleep or make you wild for my bod."

Charlie got rid of the robe. "I'm already wild for your bod. How much wilder do you want?"

"Lie on your stomach first," he instructed, and when she did, he squirted a gob of lotion onto her back.

"That's cold!" Charlie yelped.

"Complaints, complaints," Cole groaned. "All I get are complaints." He bent down and bit her shoulder playfully. "Any more complaints and you'll get a lot worse than that," he threatened.

Charlie giggled, and heard herself with dismay. She never giggled. She laughed, she roared sometimes, but she never giggled, and that had definitely been a giggle. "Get on with your back rub," she ordered with mock ferocity.

Cole began to stroke the lotion into her skin. "You think this is an ordinary back rub? Sweetheart, you're in for the surprise of your life."

Her eyes closed. "Whatever you call it, it feels wonderful."

"Do you know you have some tight muscles back here?"

"What are you, a masseur on the side?"

Cole chuckled. "And I thought I had just taken all the tension out of you. Looks like you need another dose of Uncle Cole's cure-all."

"Which is?" she asked, hearing a more relaxed tone in her voice. Cole's hands were incredible, moving slowly up and down her back, lingering at apparent kinks here and there.

He bent over and kissed the side of her neck. "What do you think?" he growled in exaggerated wolfishness.

"Oh. Well, I should have known." She was getting drowsy. She'd never had a back rub in her life and to be experiencing her first at the hands of this man was causing the most delicious serenity she'd ever felt.

He moved lower, this time squirting the lotion on his hands and warming it before applying it, and his movements over her buttocks and thighs were hypnotizing. Charlie sighed with utter contentment.

"Like that?"

"It's pure magic," she breathed.

He did her calves, her feet, and Charlie was very close to oblivion when he said, "Turn over, sweetheart. Now the fun begins."

She was feeling so loose she turned over in slow motion. "Fun?"

Cole filled one palm with lotion and rubbed it into his other hand. "Fun," he repeated, so erotically that Charlie's eyes opened fully. He began at her shoulders, working the silky lotion into her arms, her fingers, and now she could see his face. As before, when she'd watched him enjoy touching her, her insides turned to mush.

He caressed her breasts tenderly, sliding his hands over them again and again. Her nipples had grown firm at the first contact, and each pass he made over them sent a jolting lightning bolt through her system. She wet her lips. "Cole..."

He smiled. "Told you it was fun."

He did her waist, following its inward curve over and over, returning to her breasts, dropping downward again, going a little lower each time. "Do I get to return the favor?" she asked tremulously.

"Do you want to?"

"If I'm in any condition to do so when you're through."

"You don't seem to be falling asleep. Does that mean you're getting wild for my bod?" he teased, massaging her thighs with long, sure strokes.

"I think you know the answer to that," she moaned.

"I don't feel any tight muscles anymore."

"I'm sure you don't." God, he was tormenting her, skirting the unbelievable ache he'd created with his teasing fingertips.

Cole dried his hands on the sheet. "The rest of the massage is done without lotion," he said, lying down next to her.

Charlie looked at him with pleading eyes. "Where did you learn that technique?"

His mouth brushed hers. "Don't ask, sweetheart. Some things are better left in the deep, dark past." His expression tensed. "Don't worry, Charlie," he whispered. "Nothing I've ever done before comes close to what you make me feel." His lips came down hard.

She knew he was aroused. He'd done nothing to conceal his body during the game. The massage had worked on both of them, creating a sexuality that brought them to an explosive passion. With a frantic wild haste they made love, and when they lay gasping and spent, the peace that descended on Charlie was so perfect that she wished she could remain in it forever.

They spoke in whispers, neither wanting to shatter the moment, and Cole turned out the light and curled around her limp body, his chest at her back, his lap curved around her hips.

She was almost asleep, already dreaming, seeing a hazy, golden future with Cole, when he murmured, "I've got to be away on business for four or five days. I'm leaving in the morning."

"All right." She sighed drowsily.

"I'll call."

"Yes," she agreed with eyelids too heavy to keep open any longer.

And then she heard—or dreamed—"I love you, Charlie," a whisper in the night, a flutter of butterfly wings, a dream, a beautiful dream…in and out of her mind. She was fast asleep.

CHARLIE CALLED ROGER COOK the next morning. "I think you know I'm anxious about the possible trade, Roger. I'd like your permission to take a logger, George Morrison, out to the Copley property."

"I don't see any reason why the Copleys would object," Roger readily agreed.

"Thanks. This might be putting the cart before the horse, but I really want George's input on the timber."

"I understand, Charlie. You do whatever you think best."

Following her chat with Roger, Charlie called George Morrison and asked him to accompany her to the property. George had logged for the McAllisters off and on for years, and he was happy to hear from Charlie. Inordinately happy, she thought. "You've been logging for Canfield, haven't you, George?"

"Yeah. And I don't mind telling you I'd just as soon be doing something else," George replied, sounding grim, Charlie thought.

Charlie had a feeling George's attitude had something to do with working under Rick Slaughter, but she didn't pursue the subject. They arranged a drive to the property that afternoon and Charlie hung up, satisfied that things were moving along nicely.

Actually, Cole's business trip couldn't have been better timed if she had planned it. His absence gave her all the room she needed for the many details to take care of this week, without having to hedge around with feeble excuses about what she was doing.

It wasn't wrong to keep it from Cole, Charlie assured herself repeatedly. There was no point in arguing over something that might not reach fruition. If and when the trade was agreed upon, she would gladly tell him everything. In the meantime it made sense to get her ducks in a row. George Morrison's expertise was very important to the deal. He was the man to tell her if she could log the property without involving Canfield, which was what Charlie had decided she would prefer doing. It was all that oversized timber on the Copley property that had her worried, and she ardently hoped George would tell her they could take the small timber and forget the large.

Sitting back, Charlie turned her thoughts to last night and how wonderful it had been. Cole's face and body filled her mind. He was beautiful. And intelligent and sensitive and...

She blinked and sat up straighter. Wasn't she blaming him for the past any longer? Charlie thought about it—seeing Cole in such a different light startled her. The way she felt now made her original opinion appear narrow and hasty. Her spirit soared every time she thought of Cole now, and there was something else, too, something that had happened last night and kept eluding her, something to do with Cole.

She couldn't quite grasp it, but it gave her a warm, lovely feeling, and she concentrated on the dreamlike sensation until Joan came in with a question, bringing her back down to earth and the reality of the office.

It was a little later that it occurred to Charlie to wonder why she hadn't felt any repercussions from the gossip Rick had probably spread around about her and Cole. Not that anyone would approach her straight out with it. But her friends weren't above some good-natured ribbing, and so far she hadn't picked up even a hint that anyone knew Rick had caught her and Cole in a compromising situation. And she'd been so sure Rick would delight in spreading the news.

Maybe there was just no understanding Rick, either in his business tactics or his personal habits. Not that she wanted to understand the man. Imagining a circumstance where she might want anything to do with Rick was nearly impossible, and certainly nothing she wanted to dwell on.

GEORGE MORRISON WAS somewhere between fifty and sixty years of age, a barrel-chested man with the stamina and bull-strength of a man twenty years younger. He and Charlie hiked through the two hundred acres and she was winded long before George was.

The logger made it clear that he thought the timber was outstanding. "With proper reforestation, Charlie, you could have timber here forever," he told her.

"This is much better than my section ever was, George."

"A lot better." George had logged that section of land for Charlie and knew how sparse the timber had been. Here the trees were thick and lush. "If you take the older trees first..."

"But they're the largest," she protested. "I can't cut them in my mill."

"All I can tell you is, log this land right and you'll never be out of timber again. That's my advice, Charlie, for what it's worth."

She chewed her bottom lip thoughtfully. "It's worth a lot," she replied, envisioning a peaceful future without timber worries. But it would mean striking a deal with Cole. She would have to sell the large timber to Canfield.

What if Cole refused to buy it?

Was there a chance of that?

Charlie's stomach turned over. George was right; she knew he was. But going to Cole with a plea to help her out on the Copley deal so she could cancel their contract wasn't a pleasant prospect. Well, she would have to do it. What choice did she have? It would have been a little easier to talk about it on the phone if she'd mentioned the trade before he left, but she'd had such high hopes of getting a different report from George. Now she had to involve Cole in the very deal itself. Damn!

ROGER CALLED THAT EVENING with more dire news. "The Copley brothers are coming on Thursday instead of the weekend, Charlie."

"Thursday! But that's tomorrow, Roger."

"Sure is. Hey, I thought you'd be glad."

Glad? How was she going to wire this thing together without talking to Cole first? What if the Copleys insisted on an immediate decision? Dare she make the trade without securing a home for that oversized timber? George had patiently explained the waste of time and money it would be to take only the small timber off the property, impressing on Charlie the need to log it properly to ensure an endless future supply of raw material for her mill. She simply had to talk to Cole about it before she met the Copleys.

But they were coming tomorrow, and Cole hadn't called.

Could she locate him? Frowning, Charlie wondered about Cole's secretary. She would know where he was. Dammit, why hadn't she at least asked Cole where he was going? And who was Cole's secretary, anyway? How could she reach the woman tonight when she didn't even know her name?

Everything was happening too soon. If the Copleys hadn't changed their schedule, Cole might have returned before she was faced with the final stage of the trade. He'd said four or five days, hadn't he? That would put him back in the area on the weekend. Oh, damn, what a mess this was turning out to be.

Roger went on. "I'm picking the Copleys up at the Missoula airport in the morning and taking them directly to your property, Charlie. We should have an answer by tomorrow night. I'll let you know."

Charlie put the phone down and chewed on a thumbnail. This was her big chance and nothing was going right. What if Cole didn't call until tomorrow night? If only she had some sense of what he would do.

Rick Slaughter would know if Cole was interested in more timber. But how could she call and ask that snake? Just the thought of it made Charlie shudder.

She groaned out loud and got up to pace her living room. *Think*, she commanded herself. *Think this thing through!*

Before Cole had moved to the area, Rick had bought every piece of timber he could get his hands on. And if he got a look at the Copley property, he'd probably drool over those large, beautiful trees. But what would Cole say if Rick agreed to buy *her* timber? That was the rub. If it was anyone else's timber but hers, Cole would only be thrilled to add it to his inventory.

That's all she wanted, Charlie realized, a commitment from someone in authority at Canfield. That meant either Cole or Rick. And Cole was gone.

Oh, why hadn't she mentioned the trade before he left? Yes, it might have created some dissension, but what did her alternative involve? The Copley's unexpected haste had thrown everything off schedule. Would Cole understand that when he returned and learned she had not only secured some timber of her own, but she had gotten a commitment from Canfield to buy the oversized trees via Rick?

He'd do it, Charlie knew. Rick would jump at the opportunity to get hold of that oversized timber. She was the one who had a problem with it. The man had practically admitted responsibility for that second fire and threatened her to boot. He should be in prison rather than representing a company like Canfield. When Cole got back she was going to tell him what Rick had said that day. It was one more thing she shouldn't have remained silent on.

The phone rang and Charlie leaped across the room, positive it was Cole. But it was Cassie's voice. "Charlie?"

"Oh, Cass, it's you," she said dejectedly.

"Well, thanks, sis."

"No, no, I didn't mean that the way it sounded. I was expecting another call."

"Should I hang up?"

"Of course not. I'm glad you called."

Cassie sighed. "Well, I have a problem."

Oh, no! Did she have the energy for one more problem? "What is it?" Charlie asked quietly.

"Jim asked me to move in with him."

Charlie's heart sank. "Do you want me to tell you to do it, Cass?" she asked, a bit sharper than she'd intended.

"I caught you at a bad time, didn't I?"

Sighing, Charlie calmed herself. "I'm in a state, but it has nothing to do with you."

"What's wrong, Charlie?"

"Everything...nothing." Charlie realized she didn't want to explain the very complex situation. Maybe the Copleys wouldn't even like the McAllister property and this would all be over. Some deep, unhappy part of herself almost wished they would say no. "I'm sorry I was short, Cass. Tell me about you and Jim."

A pause preceded "I'm in love with him, sis. We love each other."

"And you're thinking of living together." What happened to marriage? Charlie thought sadly. Dammit, what happened to people in love getting married?

Well, she had no room to talk. Wasn't she as deeply involved with a man as a woman could get without a wedding ring? What if Cole asked her to move in with him?

No way, she decided vehemently. But she wasn't Cassie. And the eight years between their ages could almost constitute a generation gap. Cassie saw things differently than she did. In many ways, she always had. "Cass, it's your decision. Do you really want my opinion?"

"You don't approve."

Charlie thought about it again. "Maybe not. But maybe that's not important. Follow your heart, Cass. That's all I can tell you."

Cassie sighed. "Well, I haven't said yes and I haven't said no. Maybe I'll think about it some more."

Charlie prowled the house until eleven, then climbed the stairs to go to bed. If Cole didn't call in the morning, she had no choice but to contact Rick.

JUST AS CHARLIE turned off the shower the next morning, she heard the phone ringing in her bedroom. Grabbing a towel, she dripped water through the hall in a dash to reach the phone in time, praying it was Cole. Her lunge at the phone was frantic, but too late. Whoever it was had hung up. All she heard was the drone of the dial tone.

It was early, just a little after five, and no one local called at that time of the day. It had to have been Cole. And she had missed his call because of that damned shower! It had happened before, and several times she'd thought of having a phone installed in the bathroom. But until now the few calls she'd missed hadn't been that crucial, and she'd procrastinated.

Charlie rubbed her eyes wearily. Last night had been horrible, filled with worry and restless dreams, and now this. Talking to Cole was so important it made her ill to contemplate the results of *not* talking to him. She could explain everything, of course, and she would try. But what if he took it all wrong? She'd had the perfect opportunity to tell him about the trade on Tuesday night, and she hadn't taken it. The whole thing looked underhanded, even to her, and she knew how sincere her intentions had been. What would it look like to Cole?

At her desk later, Charlie dialed Canfield's number. Not to talk to Rick, either. She'd decided that approaching Rick was only a last resort, a final effort should all else fail, and when a Canfield receptionist came on the line, Charlie asked for Cole Morgan's secretary.

A pleasant female voice said, "Cole Morgan's office."

Charlie introduced herself and explained, "It's imperative I speak to Mr. Morgan this morning. He told me he would be away for a few days, but I don't know how to reach him. Can you give me that information?"

"Yes, of course. Mr. Morgan is in Washington, D.C. He's staying at the Hilton Hotel.

Weak with relief, Charlie scribbled the phone number on a pad and thanked the woman. Then she dialed Washington, D.C. The hotel operator put the call through to Cole's room without delay, but it rang and rang with no response.

"I'm sorry, but that room doesn't answer," the operator said.

"May I leave a message?"

"Certainly."

"Have Mr. Morgan call Charlotte McAllister as soon as possible. It's very important." Charlie thought Cole might have her number with him, but she gave the operator both the mill's number and her home number, just in case.

Then, after she'd hung up, she sat back. All she could do was hope Cole called before Roger did. It was going to be a long day.

CHARLIE STAYED in the office, determined not to miss another attempt on Cole's part to reach her. As the hours passed, though, a feeling grew that he wouldn't try again until that evening. By four she was sure of it, and by five she realized the worst had happened. If she didn't catch Rick Slaughter at Canfield before he left for the day, she would have to deal with the Copleys without any sort of commitment on that large timber.

Her skin crawled at the mere thought of dealing with Rick, but the success of the trade depended on selling that large timber. Cole would understand that necessity, she felt, even if he was furious over her reticence before he left. Even if Cole had been aware of the deal, she might have had to deal with Rick anyway. Hadn't Cole said that Rick handled everything that had to do with timber for Canfield?

Admitting she was grasping at straws, and feeling queasy over it, Charlie dialed Canfield's number again. Rick's voice on the phone choked her, but she managed a reasonably calm reply. "Rick, this is Charlie McAllister."

The phone went absolutely dead for a beat, then she heard him drawl sarcastically. "Well, now, isn't this a surprise? To what do I owe the honor?"

"Business," she intoned. "Are you interested in some exceptionally good timber?"

Suspicion entered his voice. "Where'd you get some exceptionally good timber, Charlie? I thought you were cutting our small logs."

"I am. But I found an excellent stand of timber."

"Where?"

Oh, no, you don't, Charlie thought wryly. She wouldn't put it past Rick to try and slither into her deal if he knew the details. "That's not important at this point. What is important is whether or not Canfield would be interested in buying the oversized timber."

"Because you can't cut it in your mill," Rick returned triumphantly.

"That's right," she admitted, wincing at the superiority of Rick's position. She had a product, but he had the buying power.

He stopped crowing and asked, "How come you're going behind Cole's back on this?"

"I'm not!" she gasped. "I'd be talking to him if he was here."

"You in a hurry or something?"

There was no point in lying. "Yes. Time is important," she conceded, nodding to herself, reassuring herself it was true. Time *was* important. She would feel a lot more secure exchanging six hundred acres for two hundred acres if she had the large timber sold.

"Well, now, I might need to think about this some. How much timber are you talking about?"

Charlie told him and Rick whistled. "That is a find! How'd I miss it? I thought I knew every piece of available timberland in the area."

"I'm sure I don't know," Charlie said dryly, taking a momentary pleasure out of having bested Rick at least once. "Are you interested?" she pressed, anxious to get this over with.

"I'd have to see the timber before I could say."

"Are you turning it down?"

"Nope. I just wanna see it."

Charlie paused. "Look, all I need is a commitment based on my word that the timber is sound. That doesn't worry me because I know how good it is. Is Canfield buying timber as usual? That's all I'm asking."

"How come you didn't talk to Cole about this before he left?"

"Because I wasn't sure of it, that's why!" she snapped.

"And he doesn't know anything about it?"

Impatience made Charlie grimace and roll her eyes. "Not yet," she responded sharply. She could almost hear Rick's wheels turning. What concerned her was their direction. She couldn't second guess Rick Slaughter no matter how she might try, and she didn't trust him as far as she could throw him. "Can you give me an answer?" she urged.

"I can, but I'm thinking."

Charlie waited, then snapped, "Dammit, Rick! You know the answer to my question without dragging this out for an hour."

"My, my, aren't you the impatient one. Tell you what, babe, you meet me someplace and we'll talk about it."

Charlie saw red. "Forget it! I'll wait for Cole!" She slammed the phone down hard enough to break it in two, then grabbed her purse and stormed out of the office.

11

IT KEPT GNAWING at Charlie while she drove home that she was in exactly the same sort of quandary she had feared would happen if she mixed business with her personal life. She wouldn't be taking this emotional drubbing and living on the brink of nausea if she wasn't so worried about how Cole might take all this. Independence was assuming a new aspect. Before falling for Cole, all she'd thought of was becoming a free agent again. The more involved she became, the more her image of independence blurred. She wasn't even sure what it meant anymore, except for one very clear point: she didn't want it to mean being alone again, not after a taste of what togetherness really meant. She was afraid of losing Cole, plain and simple.

She and Cole were so well suited, Charlie realized poignantly, and not only in the bedroom. Her feelings went far beyond physicality. She was in love with him—hopelessly, deeply in love with him.

Charlie's shoulders slumped as she let out a deep sigh. Why should she feel so despondent about being in love? She should be ecstatic, like Cassie.

No, Cassie wasn't ecstatic anymore, either. She'd been that way over the Fourth of July weekend, but she, too, had problems to iron out now. Was love always like this? Heartrending? Confidence-stealing? Maybe that was the difficult part of this whole thing, Charlie acknowledged sadly. She had no confidence she was doing the right thing anymore. Worry concerning Cole's reactions was taking precedence.

Charlie pulled into her driveway, got out of the pickup and walked with a dejected gait to the house. She could barely tolerate thinking about the telephone conversation with Rick, but it was part of the general dissatisfaction she was suffering. Calling Rick had been a dreadful mistake, but maybe nothing else would have pointed out more clearly how disorganized her thoughts were these days.

With one foot on the porch, she heard the telephone ringing in the house. Her pulse leaped, and she unlocked the door and sprinted to the nearest phone, the one in the kitchen. "Hello?" she said breathlessly.

"Charlie? Roger Cook."

She'd been so sure it was Cole, she felt like crying. But Roger's call was important, too. "Yes, Roger," she said, putting enthusiasm in her voice.

"They like it, Charlie. They like it a lot."

Despite all the pressures and problems of the day, Charlie breathed a big sigh and smiled. "That's great, Roger."

"Listen, we're at Potter's Café. The Copleys want you to join them for dinner. I told them that shouldn't be a problem."

Cole might call! Charlie's smile faltered. "I'm expecting an important phone call, Roger. Could we do this in the morning?"

"No, sorry. They're leaving on a nine o'clock flight tonight. They've got their deed with them, ready to sign it over. I think if you want the deal, you better get over here. And bring your deed with you."

So fast? Charlie hesitated, her mind racing. Cole might call while she was gone, but even that concern was overshadowed by the fact that once she exchanged deeds, that was it. In the realm of commitments, this was major. Cassie wouldn't mind, Charlie knew; she'd always left the business strictly up to Charlie. Besides, the trade would benefit Cassie financially the rest of her life. *If* Charlie got the large timber sold so George Morrison could log the Copley land properly.

Well, she'd started this thing, and what choice did she have but to see it through? It wasn't the Copley's fault she was in a dither over the big timber on their land.

"All right, Roger. Give me half an hour, okay?"

"Sure. We'll have some coffee while we wait."

IN A COMFORTABLE HOTEL ROOM in Washington, D.C., Cole held the phone to his ear through eight rings, then put it down with a frown. He'd tried to reach Charlie last night and gotten only a busy signal—twice. Then, this morning, there'd been no answer at her house, even though by Montana time it had been a very early hour. Now, this evening, there was no answer again.

He only had a few minutes before he had to leave again— the meetings he'd come for had been incessant and demanding—but he hurriedly dialed McAllister Lumber Company's phone number again. While the phone rang, he eyed the message he'd received.

Important you call Charlotte McAllister as soon as possible!

Cole had come back to the hotel for a shower and a change of clothes and had been given Charlie's message when he came in. He was attending a conference of lumber-industry lobbyists, and the conference's planners had allowed very little time between almost continuous meetings that were of great consequence to lumbermen across the nation. Tariffs on imports and exports had been discussed, and proposals for new laws had been sweated over. On top of those very serious events, dinners with important people in the industry had been scheduled for every night of his stay.

He had no time for busy signals and unanswered phone calls, and it annoyed him that Charlie was so hard to reach. It also worried him.

Where had she been all day Tuesday that she hadn't returned his calls and then had gotten home so late? She sure had avoided an explanation. At the time he'd overlooked it, thinking she had a right to her privacy. But now, after two days without contact, he was beginning to wonder.

And, dammit, if it was important she talk to him, why wasn't she near a phone?

Cole slammed his phone down. He had to go. But a premonition told him something was wrong in Montana, and Charlie was involved in it, whatever it was, right up to her pretty green eyeballs!

WHEN CHARLIE GOT BACK HOME from Potter's Café she went directly to the telephone and dialed Cole's hotel again. She was pretty sure it was three hours later in Washington, which would make it ten-thirty there, and she was hopeful she'd catch Cole in his room.

This time when there was no answer she didn't leave a message.

Recognizing a developing anger that Cole hadn't even tried to reach her at the mill all day, she put a call through to Cassie. And after telling her sister all about the land trade, she expressed doubts as to the wisdom of her move. "It's going to come between Cole and me," she said in an oddly resigned voice.

"Why is everything always so complicated?" Cassie sighed.

"I wish I knew," Charlie replied. "If I could have talked to him before I met the Copleys..."

"What's he doing in Washington, sis?"

"He didn't say."

"I wish I could be cheerier, but I've got a decision to make, too."

"Yes, I know."

Later Charlie tried Cole's hotel again, putting through a person-to-person call to avoid charges if he wasn't there. The operator cut her off with "I'm sorry. Your party doesn't answer."

The evening dragged and it was hard to stay calm. She didn't like herself this way, undecided, at odds, tripping over her own emotions, and it wasn't difficult to lay the blame on Cole. She'd never had trouble making business decisions before, and she wondered how a romantic involvement with a man could influence her very personality so much.

When the phone rang at nine she rushed to it as though it were suddenly going to sprout legs and run away. "Hello?" she cried.

"Charlie? Cole. You're damned hard to catch these days. What's going on?"

The anger that had been lurking on the edges of her consciousness exploded. "*I'm* hard to catch!" she yelled. "You're the most elusive person I've ever known."

"I happen to be extremely busy. This isn't a vacation I'm on."

Charlie struggled for calmness, and she succeeded to a point. At least she wasn't yelling now. "No? Well, I wouldn't know about that, would I? I don't recall your explaining anything about this trip."

"Do you want an explanation? I'm very willing to explain. I'm here for a conference on the status of the lumber business in this country today. We need some tougher laws, maybe higher tariffs on imports. That's what I've been working on. What've you been doing?"

He was angry, too. Maybe not yelling, but he was angry enough to speak with unaccustomed sarcasm. Charlie heard it and resented it. "I was at the mill all day, hoping you'd call," she snapped.

"And this morning at five o'clock?"

"That *was* you. I happened to be in the shower and got to the phone too late." Anger was getting them nowhere. Charlie took a deep breath. "Cole, I have to talk to you about something. Did you get a message that I called this morning?"

"Yes. I tried to call you back around five-thirty your time. You weren't at home or at the mill."

"I've been busy, too."

"So I gathered. Doing what?"

They still weren't being nice to each other. It was apparent to Charlie that Cole was as upset over not reaching her as she'd been over not reaching him. This wasn't a very good time to spring her news, was it? And what good would it do now, anyway? The trade had been made, there was no turning back, and if Cole said no to buying her large timber, she'd just have to make the best of it.

"When will you be back?" she questioned.

"The conference is officially over Friday night. I should be back on Saturday."

"Maybe it would be best to wait until then to talk. It's too late to do anything about it now, anyway."

"Too late? I knew something was going on. Explain, Charlie."

"You're really angry with me, aren't you? Why? I've been waiting and hoping you'd call for two days."

She heard only a heavy silence for a few moments, then a deep, masculine sigh. "You're right. I'm sorry. Obviously we just kept missing each other. You worry me, though, Charlie. I have a feeling something's going on there that I should know. Are you going to tell me about it?"

"It is something you should know, Cole. I should have told you before you left," she said softly, suddenly shaken by the change in his voice. She mirrored Cole's emotions, Charlie realized. If he was angry, she was angry; if he was loving and sweet, her insides turned to jelly.

"I'm listening."

Charlie braced herself. "I traded a section of my land for a very good two hundred acres of timberland."

She wasn't prepared for the weary "I see" she heard.

"Is that all you have to say?" she questioned anxiously.

"What do you want me to say? It's what you've wanted all along. Maybe I've been expecting it. Charlie, I'm beat. It's midnight here and I've been on the go since six this morning. We'll talk about it when I get back."

He wasn't even going to discuss it with her. Charlie's chin quivered, but she ignored the weepy urge and squared her shoulders. "I'm sorry I bothered you with my insignificant little problems," she said coolly.

"Dammit, don't take that attitude! Your problems aren't insignificant to me."

"Yes, they are. You're much more concerned with the state of the lumber industry as a whole than you are with what's gone on in your own backyard. Why hasn't it occurred to you that people like your timber supervisor do as much damage to the lumber industry as too much foreign import? It's very hard for me to visualize you poring over bills and laws to prevent generalized production decreases when you don't give a personal damn what happened right here in Montana!"

"Are we back to that?"

"Maybe we are. Then again, maybe we never really got away from it. Good night, Cole."

Later in bed, staring at the moonlight and shadows flickering across her bedroom ceiling, Charlie went over the conversation again. She made excuses for Cole's anger, and for her own. She admitted she'd been short-tempered and resentful, and she allowed Cole's right to be tired and impatient. But something had gone out of their relationship tonight, and Charlie wondered if it could ever again be the same as it had been before they'd finally made long-distance contact.

CHARLIE COULD HARDLY believe it when Rick Slaughter sauntered into her office the next morning. Nor that he plopped down in a chair across her desk without an invitation. "I've been thinking about that timber you offered to sell Canfield, Charlie. I wanna take a look at it."

"Sorry," she said icily. "I won't deal with you."

"No? What do you propose to do? Sit on all those over-sized trees?"

"What I do with them is no concern of yours. When Cole gets back I'll talk to him."

Rick smirked. "It is my concern. You seem to have forgotten that I'm Canfield's timber supervisor. Cole leaves everything in the timber department up to me. If you want to sell that timber, you'll have to deal with me, like it or not."

Charlie sat back. That possibility had occurred to her only yesterday, but some deep-down hope had made her feel that Cole would give her timber special and personal attention. This morning she wasn't so sure.

Rick took advantage of her hesitancy. "Show it to me, Charlie. I'll pay top dollar if it's as good as you say."

She chewed her lip. Last night's long-distance quarrel had been irrational and a cruel trick of circumstance, but it still hurt that Cole hadn't allowed her to explain the land trade. "We'll talk about it when I get back" had been a pretty weak response to something she had lost sleep and suffered over.

Maybe he didn't care what she did!

Charlie's heart kicked up at the frightening new thought. Maybe she'd been kidding herself about the seriousness of their personal involvement. Maybe she'd worried herself sick about nothing!

Charlie's eyes narrowed at Rick. Yes, it was entirely possible that Cole would turn her timber transaction over to Rick—very likely, in fact. If she wanted to sell that large timber, she was going to have to deal with this weasel, whether Cole was back or not.

There was no point in delaying the inevitable. The sooner she made a deal with Canfield, the sooner she could get George Morrison logging her land. And the sooner she had her own log supply again, the sooner she could give Cole notice that she was canceling their contract. It was a crazy, convoluted situation and it bothered her even if it rolled off Cole like water off a duck's back.

Why had she been so worried about what Cole might think of her deal? He probably didn't give a damn about it any more than he gave a damn that this snake in man's clothing sitting now in her office had all but eliminated the lumber industry in western Montana. There was little Rick Slaughter wouldn't do, Charlie realized as she remembered how her lumber had gone up in smoke. The man was capable of anything, and Cole refused to see it.

She rose, angry with the weight of having to do business with this man. "I'll show you the timber this afternoon."

A smug smile broke out on Rick's face, and he got up, too. Charlie ignored the irritating grin and stated, "I'll meet you at the Troutdale turnoff right after lunch. You can follow me to the property in your truck."

"I can't do it until four."

"Why not?"

"I've got a logger coming in for a meeting, that's why not. I'll meet you at four."

Four was cutting it short. By the time they got back to town it would be dark. Charlie wondered if Rick really had a meeting or was just throwing his weight around again. "All right, four at the Troutdale turnoff," she agreed, just barely keeping her dislike of the man in check.

After Rick left, Charlie got herself busy. She was not going to sit around and worry anymore. When Cole returned, she hoped they would talk, but she was through making excuses for only conducting her business as she saw fit. Would she dare question a decision of his regarding Canfield? Not on a bet!

As for Rick, Charlie was positive he'd want the timber once he saw it. It was prime grade, and while not virgin, hadn't been logged for at least fifty years. Any timberman would want it. Cole would want it, for that matter. He'd probably pat Rick on the back for buying it.

At three-thirty Charlie got in her pickup and drove to the appointed spot. At ten after four Rick arrived, and she didn't even give him a chance to get out. She immediately drove off, and he followed.

They reached the property at five-thirty, and Charlie parked in a wide spot in the road and got out. Rick was already out, walking around with his eyes glued to the dense stand of timber surrounding them. "It's good stuff, all right," he conceded. "How'd you get hold of it?"

There was no reason to evade his curiosity now. "I traded my logged-off section for two hundred of these acres."

Rick eyed her with grudging respect. "Pretty shrewd, Charlie."

"So, what do you think?"

"I'd like to drive some of these old roads."

"Rick, it's all the same!"

"Then you won't mind if I look, will you?"

Charlie released an exasperated breath. "Go ahead and look. I'll wait here."

It was an hour before Rick came back, and Charlie's watch read six-forty. It would be dark for sure when they got back to town, and they still hadn't discussed price. "It is worth top dollar," she said, hoping to open the subject.

Rick rubbed the back of his hand across his mouth. "Sure could use a beer. Tell you what, Charlie. We'll drive back to town and stop at the Buckhorn to talk about it, okay?"

Her eyes narrowed. "Let's talk about it right here."

Rick grinned infuriatingly. "A man can't discuss money with a dusty throat."

How about no throat? she wanted to scream, willing to throttle this jerk on the spot. "All right, but let's get going."

"Got a date?"

Charlie flushed. "No, I don't have a date."

"Oh, I forgot. Your boyfriend's out of town, isn't he?"

"You should know. He's your boss," she snapped, climbing into her pickup and slamming the door.

Rick was going to make this as painful as possible, she realized on the drive back to Gibbs. Well, let him have his infantile fun. She could bear it a little longer, and then it would be over. Once the price was agreed upon, it would all be over.

The Buckhorn had about a dozen cars parked by it, certainly nothing like it had been the night of the Fourth. But it was busy enough that Charlie winced at the thought of walking in with Rick.

He pulled his pickup truck right up next to hers and got out, standing by while Charlie climbed down. "Rick, can't we handle this some other place?"

"Your house?" He grinned.

"Of course not my house!" It was hopeless. She followed him in and smiled weakly at a few friends.

Rick brought her to an isolated table and called for a couple of beers. He leaned back importantly, raising the hairs on Charlie's neck with a very pointed leer at her breasts. "You sure got a figure, Charlie."

"Let's talk timber prices," she said coldly.

"Miss Ice-in-her-veins McAllister. Guess Morgan thawed some of that frost, huh? How come, Charlie? Do you only go for guys with dough?"

Her green eyes were as icy as he'd accused. "I'm not going to sit here and be insulted, Rick. Either get to the subject we came here to talk about, or I'm leaving."

He looked away with a show of disgust. "All right, all right. Don't get your dander up."

Two glasses of beer were delivered, and Rick took a long pull. "Ah, that's good. All right, let's get to the point since you're so anxious." He leaned forward, speaking lower suddenly. "I've got a little proposition, Charlie, one that will make us both some money."

"I'm listening."

"Good. Like I said before, I always felt you were a pretty smart cookie. I'm going to recommend Canfield buy your timber, and believe me, what I say goes in the timber department."

"I believe you." Why wouldn't she? She had Cole's own defense of this worm as evidence.

"You'll be paid the top dollar I promised, but you'll pay me ten dollars a thousand board feet for every stick."

She stared blankly. "Pay you ten dollars a thousand? What for?"

"Think about it. I'm sure it'll come to you."

Charlie sat back, stunned. "A kickback. You want a kickback."

"See? I told you it would come to you."

This wretched piece of garbage had the nerve to steal from Cole . . . and look her in the eye while he gloated over it! So that was his game. Was he doing this to the loggers, too? With the other private timber he'd purchased for Cole? My God, he must be taking in thousands of dollars, uncountable thousands!

Not only that, he had the entire timber industry in the area in the palm of his hand. He not only had Cole believing he was wonderful, he had run all the other small mills out of business, putting him in the position of manipulating every timber deal that went on. What a blow it must have been to have Cole "save" her business by offering her that contract!

And even after torching her property, he'd gotten so smug he was daring to ensnare her in his crooked schemes!

Charlie's mind raced, and everything was so clear she wondered why she hadn't seen it before. Why hadn't someone exposed this crook? Why would people allow him to bleed them?

Oh, yes, the reason was simple. With the loggers, anyway. If they wanted to work, they paid Rick. Was that why George Morrison was so thrilled to quit working for Canfield? As for landowners in her present position, if they wanted to sell a large block of timber that she and the other small-mill owners couldn't afford, they went to Rick and he made them this kind of offer. Take it or leave it.

Charlie was so furious her skin had paled several shades. "You miserable, slimy bastard," she said through clenched teeth. "I wouldn't take your deal if—"

She saw Rick's gaze jerk upward and a sickly grin appear on his face. "Cole! Hey, you're back early. Great! I was just—"

Charlie whirled and jumped up. "Cole!" Her chair fell backward and hit the floor with a bang. Cole kept looking from Rick to her, and his face was dark with repressed anger. "What's going on here?"

Rick was babbling, and people were looking, and Charlie tried to make a coherent sentence. It came out something like "My timber . . . Copley property . . . Canfield . . ."

Then she heard Rick saying. "Hell, Cole, she's got some pretty good timber and—"

Cole swung on her. "Why are you here with Rick?"

The whole place was quiet, with everyone watching in stunned silence. "Can we do this some other place?" Charlie asked in an undertone.

"Are you ashamed again, Charlie?" Cole taunted.

Her head jerked up. "You want to talk here? Are you sure?" Her voice was much louder. Ashamed? She'd show him who'd end up ashamed.

Rick was hovering around Cole nervously. "Come on, Cole. Let's go outside and talk."

"Yes, Cole. Take that snake outside before I pour this beer over his head!"

"What is going on?" Cole yelled.

Charlie pointed an accusing finger. "That weasel just offered to buy my timber if I paid him a ten dollar a thousand kickback!"

"That's a lie!" Rick screamed. "I'm not staying in here and listening to her lies, Cole."

Cole turned on him. "Then get the hell out!" he thundered, enunciating each syllable distinctly. He grabbed Charlie by the arm. "Come on. We've provided enough of a floor show for one night."

Charlie stumbled across the room trying to shake Cole's hand, but his fingers were wound around her arm too tightly. "You damned bully!" she shouted.

Cole stopped at the door and turned to the gaping crowd. "Good night, folks. Sorry we disrupted your evening." Then he dragged Charlie through the door and out to the parking lot.

Rick was standing by his pickup, literally hopping from one foot to the other, flagrantly uncertain what to do next. Cole let Charlie go when they got near him. "Now, suppose my girl, and my friend *and* employee, tell me what the hell they were doing out together on a Friday night!"

"Hey, Cole, it wasn't like that," Rick whined.

Shocked that Cole would even think such a thing, Charlie glared. "Don't you so much as hint that I would have anything to do with this . . . this . . ."

"Weasel?" Cole offered coldly. "What should I hint at, Charlie? What should I think when I walk into a bar and see you and Rick with your heads together?"

"We were talking business," Charlie returned coldly. "Or we were until he laid that kickback scheme on me."

Rick yelped. "Don't believe anything she says, Cole. She's always tried to make trouble for me. You know that."

Charlie looked at the two of them, and her stomach turned over. This was ridiculous. There was no way she could explain the matter to Cole with Rick pleading like the yellow dog he really was. How brave he'd been while threatening her that day, but he sure sang a different tune to Cole. "I'm going home," she declared. "Cole, you believe anything you want to. That's your choice. But if you ever trust this piece of slime again, you're a fool!"

Cole caught her arm. "I'm not a fool, Charlie. But I wonder if you didn't forget that tonight," he said in a lethally quiet voice.

"You know what I think of Rick," she spat. "Now I'd appreciate you letting me leave. If and when you want to talk, I'll be at home."

Rick was still hopping up and down. "It's a lie! It's a lie," he kept screaming.

"Oh, for Christ's sake, shut up," Cole yelled. "Charlie . . . I'll see you later."

She nodded and walked to her truck, and when she drove from the parking lot she saw Rick gesturing wildly, still trying to convince Cole she was lying.

Who would Cole believe, her or Rick?

Dammit, did she even care? This whole mess was getting her down. Maybe she was partially responsible. She never should have let Cole intimidate her to the point of keeping her plans to herself.

Well, she wasn't going to be intimidated any longer. And if Canfield didn't buy her large timber because of this, then she'd figure out something else.

12

THE MINUTE CHARLIE was in the house she went to the phone and called George Morrison. And when he came on the line, she got right to the reason for the call. "Did Rick Slaughter ever ask you for a kickback, George?"

"Charlie, I'm not sure we should be talking about this," the logger answered warily.

"Don't worry, George. Rick's little game is over. Tell the other loggers, will you? Cole Morgan knows about Rick's rotten scheme, and once he digests it, I'm sure Rick won't be in the area for long."

George breathed a sigh of relief. "Charlie, I didn't want to say anything. A lot of my friends are working for Canfield."

"I understand. Good night, George. We'll get together next week and go over the plans to log my property."

Charlie hung up and marched upstairs to the shower. When she was through, she dressed in clean jeans and a T-shirt, preferring to talk to Cole—if he came by—in regular clothing rather than nightwear.

Then she went downstairs, put on a pot of coffee . . . and waited.

HEADLIGHTS ILLUMINATED her driveway around ten, and Charlie opened the door before Cole put a foot on the porch. He looked tired, she noted. From the rumpled formality of his dark slacks and white shirt, she would have bet anything that a suit jacket and tie were in his car. The oddly distant look in his eyes gave her a chill, but with the events of the evening it was perhaps understandable. She moved back from the door. "Come in."

"Thanks."

They went to the living room. "Would you like some coffee?"

"Yes, thanks."

When Charlie returned with two mugs of coffee, Cole was standing by the fireplace. He accepted a mug with another "Thanks," and watched her sit down with hers.

For a minute it looked as if neither knew how to begin, but then Cole said, "I skipped today's conference sessions to get back early."

"Oh?"

"I was on my way home when I saw your truck at the Buckhorn." Cole moved to the couch and sat, and he kept looking at Charlie with a brooding expression.

She took a sip of coffee, deciding to let Cole lead. So much hinged on how he was taking what had happened.

"I thought you were out with Rick."

Her eyes flashed, even though she'd halfway expected something like that. "I can't believe you really thought that."

"Well, I did. I saw his pickup next to yours, but it didn't register until I walked in and you were together. Off at a table by yourselves."

"I despise him!"

Cole continued a relentless stare. "Do you, Charlie?"

A flush heated Charlie's face. "I've told you that a dozen times."

"Yes, you have. And Rick claims he doesn't like you. Yet you were together tonight. If I hadn't come back early and interrupted the two of you . . ."

The implication dangled, creating a roar of panic in Charlie's ears. Cole's initial reaction at finding her with Rick was perhaps natural, but he should be over it. He knew better. He had to know better. "I won't listen to that," she cried, and placed her mug on a table with a trembling hand. "Why would you think such a thing?"

Cole set his mug on a magazine on the coffee table and crumpled back against the sofa. He rubbed his eyes wearily. "I don't know what to think anymore."

Emotions roiled in Charlie. "Why don't you try believing me for a change?"

Cole's eyebrow shot up. "Is that the issue here?"

"Isn't it? You haven't believed me from the day we met. You've defended Rick every way possible and refused to even consider that I was telling you the truth."

"As you saw it, Charlie. Only as you saw it." Cole leaned forward. "If Rick's such a weasel, as you pronounced him several times at the Buckhorn, why were you there with him?"

"To make a deal on my timber! Dammit, you wouldn't even talk to me about it on the phone last night. That's why I called Washington half a dozen times yesterday. Then you wouldn't even discuss it, if you care to remember."

"Half a dozen times? Charlie, I got one message. That's hardly half a dozen times."

She swallowed. "I only left a message once. To be totally accurate, I called three times."

They were arguing over trivialities! How senseless. "Cole, why are we fighting? What's the real reason you're so upset?" It had to be the land trade. What other reason could he have for being angry with her? Charlie was ready to get the whole thing out in the open—very ready. She welcomed the chance to tell Cole everything, even her small deceit in keeping it from him before he left for Washington.

He looked away, then returned harder eyes to her. "I don't really know you, do I, Charlie?"

Her heart nearly stopped. "I'm not sure I understand."

His eyes narrowed. "Sharing someone's bed doesn't necessarily mean sharing anything else, does it?"

This wasn't what she had expected and it was making her nervous. Didn't he want an explanation of the property trade, or to hear the reasons why she'd moved so quickly? What had she done wrong, other than keep it from him before he left? At that point she hadn't even been sure it would go through.

"What do you think of me, Charlie?"

Bewildered, she could only stare at him.

"Go on, tell me. What do you think of me? Do you have any feelings beyond the obvious?"

"The obvious?" she echoed, weak with confusion.

"It's been obvious you enjoy sex with me. I don't doubt that for a minute. In bed you and I have something very special. Is that all we have, Charlie?"

This was heavy, and not at all the scene she'd envisioned. She'd been prepared to explain, then to defend her actions as her right to do business as she thought fit. Even being with Rick had had sound judgment behind it, if only Cole would let her explain.

But delving into her emotions when so much had happened was unnerving. She honestly didn't know how to answer.

"You can't even talk about it, can you?" Cole said in a low, still voice.

Images and feelings and the events of the past week raced through Charlie's mind. She remembered acknowledging how much she loved him; she remembered the pain of thinking he didn't care what she did; she remembered so much. And she didn't know why he was pressuring her about feelings now, when they'd never discussed them before. Now they should be talking about the land trade and her motivation in seeking it; they should be talking about Rick and his dirty tricks, about why Cole had been impatient on the phone last night and why she'd been upset and sharp, actualities that could be explained and apologized for. Instead he was asking her what she thought of him, and right this minute her mind was so overloaded she couldn't even think straight.

The silence stretched, then Cole shook his head. "Well, I guess there's no point in beating it to death. Like I said, I don't really know you." He got to his feet. "Thanks for the coffee."

Charlie was so stunned that she couldn't move. But as Cole reached the living-room archway, she jumped to her feet. "Are you leaving?" He couldn't! Not like this. What about Rick's duplicity? What about her timber? Would Canfield still buy it? Dammit, what about *them*?

Cole turned and rubbed the back of his neck. "I'm dead on my feet."

"But . . . what about Rick?" Anxiously Charlie clutched at his shirt sleeve.

"What about him?"

"Don't you care that he asked for a kickback?"

Cole's face was expressionless. "He says he didn't."

Charlie stepped back, anger tensing her features. "This time you don't have to take my word for it. I talked to George Morrison tonight and he said Rick's been doing the same thing with Canfield's loggers."

Cole looked as if he'd just been struck a blow. He drew a long, troubled breath. "All right. I'll look into it in the morning."

Now he was believing, but it was because of George, not her. That hurt. Charlie turned away, fighting tears. "What have I done to make you think I would lie about such a thing?" she asked hoarsely.

"What have you done to make me think you wouldn't?"

"What?" Charlie spun, immediate fury chasing the tears.

Cole's eyes were cold. "You might be one-hundred percent right about Rick, Charlie. But you had every opportunity to tell me you were planning to break our agreement. We spent most of last Sunday together, and Tuesday night as well, and we weren't in bed all that time. We talked. We talked a lot. How long have you known you would have your own timber again?"

He *was* angry about the trade! "Not that long," she cried. "It all happened so fast."

"But you did know before I left."

"I told you that on the phone."

Cole looked at her hard. "So you did. You were also pretty damned evasive on the phone. That's why I cut my trip short."

Her eyes were damp with unshed tears. "That's not fair. I tried to tell you everything. You just wouldn't listen."

Anger sparked his blue eyes. "I was exhausted! Once it sunk in . . ." He turned away. "I've had about all I can deal with for one day. I'll be in touch."

Charlie watched him go, and when the house was silent she turned off the lights and went upstairs to bed. Strangely dry-eyed, she moved much like a sleepwalker. Nothing that had happened tonight made any kind of sense at all, and she wondered listlessly if it ever would.

EVERYONE WAS TALKING about the blowup at Canfield. Charlie heard "Rick Slaughter's been fired" so many times she lost count. What affected her a lot more than all the rumors flying around, though, was Cole's silence. Days passed without so much as a phone call from him, and she began to realize that Cole had taken all that had happened as a death blow to their personal relationship.

Pete Dirksen stopped by to chuckle over Rick's discovery and to state with some smugness that he'd seen through Canfield's timber supervisor all along. "Never did like that fella, Charlie."

"He's darned lucky Morgan didn't have'm arrested," Pete declared. "Guess Morgan's just too nice a fella to have someone locked up." He chuckled again. "Bet he put the fear of God into Slaughter, though."

"I wouldn't know," Charlie replied dryly.

"Rick'll never get a decent job in the timber industry again," Pete pronounced. "Wonder if his dirty dealings were worth that."

Pete had been idling in one of Charlie's extra office chairs, and he got to his feet with an arthritic grunt. "Well, gotta go. Mave said to ask you to dinner Friday night. We got us one of those little trailers and she's having a fine old time getting it ready to roll. I think she wants you to see it."

He walked to the door and grinned with a teasing twinkle in his eye. "Besides, I have a feeling she's dying to hear what really went on in the Buckhorn the other night."

Charlie smiled weakly. "Thanks, Pete. I'd enjoy having dinner with the two of you. I'll see you Friday night."

By Wednesday morning Charlie was unhappily certain that Cole wasn't going to call at all. In spite of his promise—"I'll be in touch," he'd said—and his reference to "my girl," he'd obviously decided he didn't know her well enough to make an effort to understand why she had done what she had.

Charlie's emotions had been running the gamut about ten times a day, from deep despair to a hot, defensive anger. And in between meetings with George Morrison to get him started logging and overseeing the mill, she wondered what to do about the contract.

She thought about calling Cole to discuss it, but envisioning a completely impersonal conversation hurt too much, and she never dialed the number. She couldn't, and not only for that reason. Cole was wrong not to give her the courtesy of allowing her to explain. If any apologies were due from either of them, he owed her one a lot more than she did him. He had accused her of lying. He'd said right out that they had no relationship outside the bedroom, and to top off his heartlessness, he'd insulted her by thinking she'd been out with Rick.

Out with Rick. She'd sooner date a skunk!

Charlie had gone over the whole thing so many times she was sick of it. She was also sick over losing the Cole she'd fallen in love with, and she knew that wasn't something she'd get over quickly, if ever. Her feelings were even more deeply embedded than she'd realized. Thinking of the future without Cole gave her a terrible sense of bleakness.

But she couldn't live on lost dreams. She had a business to run, and right now her most immediate problem was the contract. Obviously she and Cole were down to nothing but business, an irony in view of that being what she had tried so hard to maintain between them in the beginning.

"Beside the point," Charlie muttered, picking up the contract to glare at it again. If all Cole wanted was a business relationship, that's what he'd get. It was time to send that thirty-day notice of cancellation. Without verbal communication she had no choice. The mill had to be ready for her own logs when they began pouring in.

"Joan?" she called. "Would you come in here, please? I need to write a letter."

TWO DAYS LATER Cole returned from a routine tour of the plant and passed his secretary on the way to his own office. "The mail is on your desk," she called.

"Thanks." Cole continued into his office and closed the door. It was Friday and he was damned glad of it. The mess with Rick, which had ultimately involved several other employees as well, had just about drained Cole, and he was looking forward to a peaceful weekend at home.

He sat at his desk, eyed the small stack of mail and decided to go through it later. Then he settled back in his chair, lifted his boots to the edge of the desk and frowned at the oil painting on the wall above a black leather couch.

What was he going to do about Charlie?

All week he'd debated the problem. All week he'd gone around in circles over it. And he no more had a solution today than he'd had on Sunday or Tuesday or yesterday. The bottom line was, he was in love with a woman he couldn't trust.

For a few minutes Cole's expression cleared while he thought of the good times they'd had together. Charlie was a hard-headed woman, but she was also the most arousing woman he'd ever known. Her body was firm and tight and soft, all at the same time, her mouth so sensual it hurt to think of it, and she responded to him with such uninhibited wildness that he knew he'd never match it no matter how many women he took to bed.

And there lay the bind: he didn't want to take any other woman to bed. He wanted to take Charlie to bed.

Cole breathed a curse and dropped his feet to the floor. Was the most meaningful sex he'd ever experienced and a gnawing need to see Charlie again enough to forget he couldn't trust her?

How could she have plotted behind his back and made love to him at the same time? Didn't she have any scruples?

She had her own timber again. Well, that was gratitude for you. He'd saved her financial butt by giving her a sweet deal and his thanks was a kick in the posterior the first chance she got. A kick he hadn't even suspected was coming.

Yes, she'd been right about Rick. She'd tried to tell him Rick was a snake all along. But she also hadn't exactly been complimentary about Cole Morgan, either, had she? At first she'd lumped him right along with Rick.

Cole rubbed the tension in the back of his neck and glanced at the mail. Might as well get it out of the way, he thought, and reached for it.

Charlie's letter was the third one down.

CHARLIE WAS EDGY all morning. It had to do with the letter and how Cole might react to it, she knew. The mill was running smoothly and Joan was handling the office efficiently, and at noon Charlie walked out of her office. "I'm going home, Joan. If you or anyone at the mill needs me, feel free to call."

"Don't you feel well, Charlie?"

"I feel fine. I just want to get out of here for a while." Charlie forced a smile. "Just hold down the fort for the rest of today, okay?"

As Charlie walked to her pickup she shot a glare toward the mill building. Even the synchronized noise she had always derived so much satisfaction from bothered her. Everything bothered her lately. The sun was too hot, the ground too dusty, the pickup needed washing. Her own body was out of rhythm, for God's sakes, like a puppet in the hands of an amateur. Nothing felt right, not one blasted thing.

She drove home with a sour expression on her face, glad she didn't have to smile for a while. She would take a long soak in the tub. Maybe that would help her mood.

A LITTLE LESS TENSE after a leisurely bath, Charlie padded around the kitchen barefoot. Clad in her nicest robe, a cream-colored silk that she refused to ruin by wearing every day and had deliberately chosen with the hope it would help chase the blues, she prepared a glass of iced tea. The phone rang.

With very little enthusiasm she picked it up. "This is Charlie."

It was Joan. "I thought you might want advance notice. Cole was just here and he's on his way to see you." Joan rushed on. "He insisted I tell him where you are. I hope you're not mad."

Mad? When every single cell in her body had suddenly been reborn?

Joan's next words brought Charlie down with a thud, though. "He's upset, Charlie. Very upset."

"Oh. Well, thanks for calling, Joan. I appreciate it."

With the phone back in its cradle, Charlie stood and thought. She was in a rather sheer robe, without a stitch on under it. She probably had another minute or so. Should she change?

Yes, of course she should. Facing an upset Cole would be bad enough without having to attempt an underdressed dignity at the same time. Charlie hurried to the stairway, but stopped at the sound of a car screeching to a halt in the driveway. Already? Cole hadn't wasted any time, had he? Her heart began an unmerciful thumping. It had been nearly a week, a horrible, unhappy week without a word from him. And now he showed up because he got her letter?

How dared he arrive like the wrath of God! Upset? Well, wasn't that just too darned bad! She was upset, too, very upset, and holding her temper in check wasn't going to be easy. Only the memory of the last time she'd screamed first and regretted it later was preventing her from planning an all-out frontal attack.

Besides, maybe her emotions were causing her to prejudge the visit unfairly. He could be upset without intending out-and-out warfare.

With forced calm, and hope in her heart, forgetting the robe completely, Charlie went to the front door at the first knock. She pulled it open and refused to be demoralized by good looks and sex appeal, although both hit her full throttle. "Hello, Cole," she said in greeting, determined to take her cue from him.

Cole felt his anger dissipate at Charlie's appearance. A robe in the middle of the day? And not just an ordinary robe, either. It wasn't quite transparent, but it was transparent enough for imaginative shadings, and his gaze dropped from neckline to hem, then raised again. He dampened his lips. "May we talk?"

Charlie studied him without a clue as to what was on his mind, other than an obvious interest in her robe! Aware of it herself, she tightened the sash at her waist.

Cole choked on the thought that any feelings she might have had for him were more than likely dead. He wasn't picking up anything from her except negativity. "May I come in?"

Charlie's heart ached. She could tell herself a thousand times that Cole owed her an apology and she might not even forgive him then, but being this close to him, hearing his voice, picking up his scent, made it hard to remain detached. "If you wish," she stated unemotionally, putting on an act she would have been proud of if she wasn't hurting so much.

They went to the living room and sat, miles apart on oppositely placed furniture. But Charlie was no more than settled when she got up again. "I forgot my iced tea. Would you like some?"

Cole stared as if slapped. Her quick rise had swirled the robe, exposing a lot of leg. He swallowed, trying to dampen his parched throat. "Yes . . . I'll have some tea," he mumbled, watching her walk from the room with swaying hips in barely-there silk. God, did she know what she was doing to him in that robe? It was odd, but he doubted it. Charlie seemed numb. Or so full of disdain for him that she couldn't have cared less how he might be feeling.

She returned with two tall glasses, and Cole stood up to accept one with a soft "Thanks." Then they both sat again.

Charlie sipped—adjusting her robe absently—and waited. When he said nothing, she asked, "What did you want to talk about?"

Cole drew a breath. "I got your letter."

"And?"

The one sharp word sounded like a dare, a crisply stated challenge. "You don't think I should be angry, do you?" he asked.

"You have no right to be. You knew the arrangement was only temporary as far as I was concerned."

How cool she was! He gave her a long, probing look. "I guess that was mentioned, wasn't it?"

"It was."

Words like deceit and deception flashed through Cole's mind. He'd had so much of that with Rick and his pals—now this thing with Charlie, while not in the same league as blackmail and out-and-out thievery, hurt a hell of a lot more. Rick was maybe Cole's own fault. He'd placed the man in a position of authority and literally given him a free hand, a necessity during his absence, but a mistake in judgment he'd be careful of in the future. It was a crying shame that trust was something you had to be careful of being too lavish with, but it was a reality.

And Charlie had proven it, too. It wasn't the fact that she'd actively sought to operate independently that hurt; it was doing so without talking about it. Did she understand that? Should he chance a battle by saying so?

He didn't want to fight with her, although he'd seen red when he'd read that letter and had started from Canfield with a few hot words in mind. But seeing her again, feeling her presence deep inside him, fighting was the last thing he wanted.

Maybe because of the robe. He hadn't expected that wisp of sexuality...and she didn't even appear to be aware of how utterly female she was in it.

"I understand you've cleared the garbage from your timber department," Charlie said tonelessly.

Cole nodded soberly. "You were right, and I was wrong. I'm sorry I doubted your word."

Charlie's eyes flashed with the first emotion she'd shown. "Nice of you to say so . . . if a little late."

"Too late, Charlie?"

Their eyes met. "Too late for what?"

Something sighed within him. It was too late. What had happened was too big, too scarring for either of them to forget. He could see it all again—his rush back because he'd sensed something wrong; spotting her truck at the Buckhorn and stopping, anxious to see her; the shock of her and Rick with their heads together, off in a corner by themselves. Then, garbled stories of timber and the deal they'd supposedly been discussing. And it had all boiled down to one thing: Charlie's inability or reluctance to trust him—her plain deceit in keeping the truth from him.

And she didn't look even slightly remorseful!

Cole's eyes narrowed. "You're finally independent again. Does it feel as good as you'd expected?"

Charlie's heart turned over. For a moment it had seemed like he was about to apologize. And she was ready to do the same. It lay on the back of her tongue—*I should have told you everything as it was happening.* But he had veered, taken another tack, and she could see he intended nothing further than what he'd already given, an apology for doubting her word. He was still supremely positive she had deliberately ignored their personal relationship.

The finality of it all made Charlie heartsick, and defensive. "It feels wonderful," she lied.

Charlie the woman, Charlie the sawmill owner . . . two different people. She had doubted he could keep business and a personal relationship separate, and she'd been right, Cole acknowledged with developing bitterness. While *she* had managed it quite well, hadn't she? To the extreme, really.

Cole got up, and when he did, so did Charlie. The robe floated gently around her ankles, a reminder of what they'd once had. For one crazy moment he thought of closing the gap between them, of forcing her into his arms, of kissing some sense into her. They'd had no problem with sex, and she could remain as cool-looking as she wanted. She had to know the pull was still breathtakingly alive. He felt it too strongly for it to be one-sided.

But what would it accomplish? When it was over they would still be the same people they were now, both full of doubt and distrust. He could see it in her eyes, he could feel it in his gut.

He turned and walked to the living-room archway.

Charlie took a step. "I'll finish cutting the logs you've already had delivered."

"Thanks, I'd appreciate that." Cole stopped and looked at her. "Maybe one thing should be said."

Hope exploded within her. "Yes?" she responded eagerly.

"We had the start of something good, Charlie. I wish you hadn't forgotten that."

Stunned, the anger Charlie had kept controlled spewed forth. "How dare you?" she ground out tensely. "I'm not the one who forgot. You are!"

Cole looked at her in amazement. Did she really see it that way? Shaking his head, he turned to leave.

Charlie didn't know whether to stop him or open the door for him. She was angry and hurt, but something important was walking out of her life and it was through a blur of tears she finally watched him go. "You stubborn...mule-headed...man," she whispered, wondering if their differences weren't as basic as that.

Regardless of how liberal attitudes had become, she was still a woman in a man's field. Analyzing the situation further, she knew Cole had acted as protector, and when she had proven she was capable of survival, and even success, on her own—without that protection—he couldn't deal with it.

If she'd been a man, he would have accepted the broken contract unemotionally. Since she was a woman...

Oh, hell, if she were a man, none of it would have happened in the first place.

DINNER AT THE DIRKSENS was great, as usual. After the meal, Mave invited Charlie to sit on the back patio. The night air was pleasantly cool, and Charlie looked up to the millions of stars with a poignant sigh, a melancholy sound Mave didn't miss.

"You're not very happy, Charlie," the astute little woman stated. "Pete thought you'd be in hog heaven now that you've got your own timber again."

"I should be," Charlie conceded with a poorly attempted laugh.

Mave patted Charlie's hand. "Your unhappiness isn't about timber, is it?"

"No, it's not."

"Are you in love with him?" Mave asked softly. "Can you talk about it?"

Charlie got up and put her hands on the patio rail. She looked off into the dark field behind the Dirksens' house. "How have you and Pete stayed happy for so long?" she said, sighing.

Mave snorted. "We've had our trials. There isn't a couple alive who doesn't have an occasional upheaval. The key is love, Charlie."

"Maybe that's the problem. Neither of us ever mentioned love. Maybe what Cole and I have . . . *had* . . . wasn't love at all. I don't know. It's just a big mess, Mave."

"But worth wading through if you think there's a chance, Charlie. This might be presumptuous, but you've never really been in love before, have you?"

"No," Charlie confessed, so low it was barely audible.

"Then don't give up without a fight," Mave said sternly. "You might be letting the real thing slip away."

"What can I do?"

"Communicate," Mave declared.

Charlie nodded sadly. "That's something we don't do very well."

"Well, it's something you have to at least try to do, my girl. You're a strong woman, Charlie. Does Cole feel threatened by that?"

"Threatened! How could he? Mave, Cole started out in life with no more than I had. He grew up around a little mill just like I did. But look what he's accomplished. I'll never have anything the size of Canfield. Why, he's a . . . a genius as far as the lumber business goes." Charlie's voice had grown stronger as she touted Cole's achievements.

Mave smiled. "Have you told him how much you admire him?"

"Well . . . no."

"Then do it. Communicate, Charlie. Communicate for all you're worth!"

13

IT WAS A SUNDAY MORNING, a dreary, heavily clouded morning that looked like an announcement for an early fall. Charlie stood at the kitchen window and stared out at the gray day. When had she ever felt more down in the dumps? she asked herself, frowning at the first drops of rain speckling the windowpane.

She had to shake this despondency. It was affecting every aspect of her life. She had little appetite, she snapped at people, getting out of bed in the morning was a chore. She was a different person than she'd been before Cole.

She had seen him face-to-face only once since his visit to the house almost two weeks ago—outside the hardware store. She'd been on her way in, he'd been coming out. "Hello, Charlie," he'd said. "Hello, Cole," she'd answered. And that had been that.

But she'd hurried through a purchase of five pounds of two-penny nails and dashed for her truck, sick at heart, so emotionally distraught she still wasn't over it. Over and over she replayed the scene. "Hello, Charlie." "Hello, Cole." Had there been even a tiny speck of warmth in his eyes?

She really couldn't go on like this, could she?

Rain was blurring the window—minute drops, a gentle shower, nothing like the fury that would strike the area later in the year. But it was enough of a storm to magnify the sorrow in Charlie's soul.

The phone rang, and with a listless sigh Charlie moved across the room to answer it. It was Cassie. After preliminaries Cassie quietly announced, "I've finally made a decision about Jim. I'm not ready for the kind of relationship he wants."

Charlie's shoulders slumped with relief.

"I still love him, Charlie. Very much," Cassie went on. "But living together doesn't seem like the right move to me. There are things we don't feel the same way about. I'm afraid if we lived together at this point our differences would be set."

"You're afraid you'd stop trying to understand each other's point of view?"

"Yes. I think we have an important relationship. But we might stifle it by not encouraging it to grow, by not asking enough of it. Do you understand?"

Charlie shook her head in amazement. "How did you get so wise, little sister?"

Cassie laughed. "Probably because of you. I don't know if I ever really said it before, but I love you dearly, Charlie. You're the wise one in this family."

Tears sprang to Charlie's eyes. "Cass . . . I love you, too, but I'm so far from wise, it's pathetic."

"Aren't things working out for you and Cole?"

Charlie gave a sad little laugh as she wiped her eyes. "We don't see each other to even try. I'm learning to live with it. It's all I can do."

"Are you sure that's all you can do? Have you tried to see him?"

"You're not suggesting I knock on his door."

"Why not? Unless you really believe he doesn't care for you . . ."

Charlie's heart turned over. "I . . . thought he did." Something flashed through her mind, the night he came to her house, the night they made love in her bed, the beautiful dreams she'd had. A deep, husky voice whispered *I love you, Charlie* in her mind.

She froze. That's what had been eluding her all this time. It *had* been a dream, hadn't it?

She could hardly speak. Her voice sounded rusty. "I thought he cared a great deal," she managed.

"Then it didn't stop because of a misunderstanding. Don't be afraid to find out for sure, Charlie. You've never been afraid of anything before. Don't start now."

For an hour after the call Charlie restlessly paced the house. Had she imagined that *I love you, Charlie*? Had it only been a part of the pink cloud she'd been floating on, something out of the deep uncertainty of her own hopes?

Or had Cole really said it and meant it and been shattered over what looked to him like deception from her?

Charlie stared at the phone with her mouth dry. If he told her no, if he said, "No, Charlie, we have nothing to talk about," could she bear it? Did it matter anymore who should apologize to whom? Wasn't she willing to do almost anything to communicate, as Mave had suggested so ardently?

She loved Cole. She would never love anyone so much. And there was a chance he loved her, too. Maybe it was too late, but could she go on into the empty future without finding out for sure?

She took a step, then another. And when she picked up the phone, she felt cold, even though she was wearing a sweater. Her fingers were stiff as she punched out the number, and the ringing of Cole's phone sounded a million miles away.

"Hello."

She swallowed. "Cole?"

Then there was silence, a painfully long silence.

"Charlie?"

She stopped holding her breath. "Yes."

"How've you been?"

"All right." No, that wasn't true. She stole a breath. "That was a reflexive answer, Cole. I haven't been all right at all."

"Why not?"

Did he care why not? Hope sprang to life. "Are you busy today?"

"Not very. Why?"

"Would you mind if I came by for a few minutes?" Charlie squeezed her eyes tightly closed. So much rested on his reply.

"I wouldn't mind at all, Charlie. I'd like to see you."

Her eyes flicked open. "Thank you. I'll see you soon."

She put the phone down. It was a beginning...and maybe nothing more. She wouldn't get her hopes too high. But she already felt a little better, didn't she? He hadn't said no.

COLE BUILT A FIRE in the living room's white quartz fireplace. The rain made it cool enough to enjoy a small blaze, and when it was burning nicely, he sat back and watched the flames.

Charlie's call had been surprising. He'd been sure she wanted nothing more to do with him. Even that day they'd run into each other at the hardware store, he'd picked nothing up from her except a haste to get away. She'd returned his hello and practically ran into the store.

His body stirred at the thought of her coming. So many, many times he'd almost gone to her house, wondering what she would do if he suddenly appeared on her doorstep. Slam the door in his face, more than likely, he'd decided.

The futility of their last meeting wasn't easily forgotten. Charlie had been cold...and so had he. There was a lot of hurt between them.

So what did she want to see him about? She still had that oversized timber, which he'd been waiting to hear about. He'd buy it, of course, but it was odd she wanted to come by on a Sunday when she could have handled it with a workday phone call.

He heard her truck climbing the bluff and got up. The rain was so fine it was almost a mist, and the forest at the back of the house was dark and dank-looking. Cole stood with the door open until her pickup stopped, then walked out to meet her. "You'll get wet," she called.

"I won't melt." She looked wonderful, beautiful, her hair in the braid but glowing in the gray light. There was tension around her eyes, though. She'd said on the phone she wasn't all right. Was there something wrong? A problem she'd decided to discuss with him?

Cole placed his hand at the small of her back and they hurried to the house. Inside, Charlie spotted the fire. "That looks inviting," she commented, the first thing she could think of to say.

They went over to the fireplace and Charlie extended her hands to the warmth, as though it were a terribly cold day and she needed the fire's heat. "Nice," she murmured.

"Sit down," Cole invited, gesturing to the twin sofas.

"Thank you." Charlie's gaze swept the room. "Looks like your decorator finished up. It's very striking, Cole."

"Glad you like it." Cole was still standing. "Coffee?"

"No, thanks. I've already got caffeine jitters from too much this morning."

"All right." He sat on the opposite couch, looking at her guardedly. "Your call surprised me."

She smiled weakly. "I imagine it did."

"I'm glad you called."

Her eyes met his. The moment of truth had come so soon. She stirred, crossing one leg over the other, and adjusted the folds of her faded denim skirt. "Thank you for saying that. These past weeks . . . well, I've wanted to call many times."

Cole leaned forward. "Why didn't you?"

She hadn't even let herself think of his good looks or that special magnetism he radiated. But now, while she looked into blue eyes with a slightly anxious cast, everything she'd been feeling and suffering for the past two weeks hit her in overwhelming waves. If she cried now she'd hate herself forever, she vowed, beating back tears by sheer willpower. "I should have," she said softly. "I'm sorry. That's what I came to say. I'm sorry for . . . everything."

Cole sucked in a breath, then got up and walked away. Charlie's eyes grew large while she watched him stop at the massive front windows, his back to her. He was wearing jeans and a white cotton sweater with the sleeves pushed up, and his tousled hair, straight back and lithe body was a lovely sight she let seep into her system.

He was having trouble with the apology, she realized with a sinking heart. She suddenly felt the urge to run, to just get up and get out of there before he gathered his thoughts enough to say something cynical, or sarcastic, or just plain hurtful.

Then, from somewhere, a spark of her old spirit came to life. Charlie recognized it with gratitude and got to her feet. "Would you rather not discuss this?" she asked, wishing her voice was just a tad steadier.

Cole was frowning when he turned around. "What do you hope to accomplish, Charlie?"

He always came from left field, didn't he? Just like that night after the scene in the Buckhorn, pinning her down on her feelings rather than encouraging an explanation. Well, she hadn't swallowed her pride and come here to beat around the bush. Her chin might be quivering a little, but it was bravely in the air. "I miss you," she said huskily. "I want us to be . . . friends again."

Cole took a step. "Just friends?"

He was giving no quarter, was he? "Lovers?" she whispered. Now he could destroy her with a word, or even a raised eyebrow. It was up to him, all up to him.

"Do you want me to make love to you? Is that why you came?"

She stared. He hadn't sounded cynical or sarcastic. He'd sounded caring, and her heart began to beat again. "I want to talk," she said thickly. "Really talk. I want to explain what I did and why I did it. I want to hear why it affected you so adversely. I want to apologize for anything I did intentionally or unintentionally."

Cole's eyes narrowed. "This is tough for you, isn't it?"

"Yes."

"And you knew it would be tough and came anyway. Am I that important to you?" While he spoke he moved closer, and when he was near enough he put a hand on her shoulder.

She wet her lips, immediately affected by the flow of electricity from him to her. "You're very important to me," she whispered.

He looked at her for an eternity, and finally said, "You're important to me, too. Let's talk." Taking her arm, he led her to the sofa. Charlie was trembling, and she gratefully sat down, noting in the haze of emotion gripping her that Cole sat very close to her.

He took her hand and looked down at it. "I've been a fool, Charlie."

She shook her head. "I fit that description much better than you," she said sadly.

He lifted his eyes to hers. "What happened? Where did we go wrong?"

Charlie sighed softly. "What did we do right? From the beginning our relationship was filled with mistrust. How could it have ended any other way?"

"It hasn't ended, has it?"

A tiny smile played across her lips. "I hope not."

"I hope not, too," Cole turned on the cushion enough to face her. "Tell me everything, Charlie."

"Yes," she breathed, hardly daring to believe the communion between them. He'd said she was important to him, too, and there was something in his eyes, a soft expression that made her heart beat faster and yet settled her nerves, too.

In a voice that started out thin and gradually gained strength, she began, going back to the years after her father died and her success with the mill. She related, chronologically, how she began to worry about timber when Rick repeatedly outbid her on government sales. She kept accusation out of her voice and recited events as they'd happened before Cole moved to the area.

"Then we met," she said quietly. "I wanted to believe you were selfish and cold-hearted. I fought so hard to keep that image in my mind. I even saw your business offer as beneficial only to you."

"Do you see it that way now?"

"Of course not. If anyone was selfish in that arrangement, it was me. I took your offer and used it to get me through a bad time. I shouldn't have accepted it, and the only thing that saved me from total insensitivity is that my crew still had jobs."

Cole's eyes roamed her face. "When did your feelings change on that, Charlie?"

"Only recently, I'm afraid. I wish I could say that I knew all along you weren't part of Rick's indifference to everyone else's well-being around here, but I didn't, Cole."

A look of misery clouded Cole's eyes. "I feel responsible for what Rick did. I never should have turned him loose like I did."

"You weren't around! How could you know what he was doing?"

"I should have." Cole looked down again, then lifted pain-filled eyes. "Charlie, I never did apologize for accusing you of being out with him that night."

Charlie shuddered. "I wouldn't have gone out with Rick if he'd been the only man in Montana. Especially after the fire."

Cole frowned. "The fire?"

Oh, yes, Charlie thought, Cole didn't know about that, did he? Well, she was determined to hold nothing back. They were talking about things they'd never dared get near before, and the fire was very much a part of their misunderstood past.

"Rick did set that fire," she said calmly, and saw the immediate doubt in Cole's eyes. "The day after he came here and realized you and I..." Charlie paused, then began again. "He stopped by the mill and told me to be very careful of what I said to you, that pillow talk sometimes gets out of hand. He said I was lucky that the fire hadn't gotten out of control, and..."

"He threatened you?" Cole looked stunned.

"Yes. I wanted to tell you, but we'd argued just the night before about Rick, and..."

Cursing, Cole jumped up and walked around. His agitation was apparent in movement and the stormy look on his face. Charlie watched with trepidation, uneasily detecting that all of Cole's upheaval wasn't caused only by Rick. She realized she was right when Cole turned and said, "And even after that, you tried to deal with him on your timber? Charlie, I'm trying awfully hard to understand, but you're a damned complex woman."

She nodded slowly. "Yes, I know that. I won't apologize for that, Cole. I am a complex person, just as you are. Do you think I could fall in love with a Simple Simon?"

Cole froze, and Charlie's face turned a bright red. She looked away from his piercing gaze, but there was no shutting out his voice. "Are you in love with me, Charlie?"

She almost asked, "Did you tell me you loved me that night we made love at my house?" But she couldn't bear another round of "You go first." Not today. Not ever again. Not with Cole. Still flushed, she looked directly into his avidly interested, vivid blue eyes. "Yes," she said distinctly. "Why else would I be here?"

He started for her, then stopped himself, eyeing her with a wise owl expression. "We're not through talking yet, are we?"

She cleared her throat, suddenly happy. "Not quite."

Nodding, Cole returned to the sofa. "Then let's get at it," he said gruffly.

Alive again, Charlie smiled. The very air had changed; the room was warmer, the gray drizzle outside only beautiful. "I want to explain," she said after letting out a breath, "why I moved so fast on my land trade."

Cole took her hand and brought it to his lips. A lingering kiss in the center of her palm created a rippling thrill throughout her body, but she tried to speak over it. "The Copleys—those are the brothers who owned the timberland—" Her breath caught as Cole began nibbling up her arm. "The Copleys came two days earlier than I'd originally been told . . ."

Her eyelids drooped with the delicious sensation of Cole's mouth on her breast. Right through her sweater and bra his breath heated her skin and brought her nipples to life. "How can I talk when you're doing that?" she whispered.

"Does it bother you?" he asked in a steamy-sounding voice.

She didn't open her eyes, and her head fell back to the sofa. "Your smallest touch bothers me," she confessed huskily, capturing his head between her hands. Her fingers caressed thick locks of his hair while he nuzzled his face into the soft swells of her bosom.

"Can we finish our talk later?" Cole murmured, then raised his head to see her.

Charlie's lashes came up and she smiled. "If you'll tell me you forgive me," she said softly.

His expression was loving. "I forgive you. Do you forgive me?"

"Oh, yes," she whispered as tears filled her eyes.

"We've wasted a lot of time, Charlie."

"I know. I made so many mistakes, Cole." She touched his face. "I want your understanding more than I've ever wanted anything," she whispered.

"We don't always think alike."

"No, we don't. I've thought about that a lot. Having differing opinions isn't what caused our problems, Cole. It's having them and letting them fester instead of getting them out in the open. I should have tried to understand your loyalty to Rick."

Cole shook his head. "You tried to tell me why you mistrusted him several times, Charlie. I had a closed mind on the man. After you blasted me that day in your office, I talked to Rick, but he lied and I let him."

Charlie smiled. "I regretted that display of temper more than you could know."

His eyes held hers. "It had to hurt you when I got so upset over finding you with Rick at the Buckhorn that night. I'm so sorry about that, Charlie."

She stroked his cheek. "Hush," she said softly. "It doesn't matter now. You believe me now, and that's all that's important. I've been miserable without you."

"I almost went to your house a dozen times."

She looked at him sadly. "We've been children, Cole."

"Yes." His head dropped to her breasts again, but it was a moment of tenderness rather than of passion. His arms curled around her and he held her, and she held him, too, and just being together like that had so much meaning. This time Charlie didn't fight the tears. She couldn't. Her heart was overflowing with love, and she gently caressed the man in her arms.

Cole raised his head and she saw mist in his eyes, too. "I love you," he said thickly. "I've loved you since the minute I saw you. I've waited for you all my life."

A sob rose in her throat. "I love you so much. I wanted to curl up and die when I thought I'd lost you."

"Oh, Charlie," he moaned, then hugged her fiercely. "What fools we've been! I'll never let you go again, ever!" His arms tightened around her even more and he captured her lips in a soul-searching kiss. When they broke apart, Cole brushed at the damp trails on her face with a thumb. "When you called, I was afraid to hope it was for any reason but business."

"I just couldn't bear it anymore. I had to try," she whispered.

"Even though you weren't sure how I'd take it. I knew it was hard for you."

She shivered. "Not as hard as living without you."

Cole released her and stood up with one hand extended. "Come on, sweetheart. Let's go find something more comfortable than this couch."

Charlie smiled all the way to his bedroom, walking on air, hardly believing she was the same woman who had awakened to such a gloomy day. Her heart sang with joy, with the certainty of their love. And while they undressed each other, adoration filled her, a feeling of oneness, a communion so pure she knew the sensation was what they had attained at moments in the past and the driving force in bringing them together again. It was what the human soul, once exposed to it, couldn't bear being without. It was the most important component of the complex emotion called love.

And they had it, she and Cole. It was something to marvel at, something to cherish and nurture and protect. Cole felt it, too. She could see it in his eyes, hear it in his whispered endearments, feel it in his touch. And the communion of sex, the giving of one's self physically, was the strongest, most expressive way to say again, "I love you." To love freely, to be able to say a thousand times, "I love you." To hear it over and over, to *feel* loved . . . Was there anything else in the world so special?

She felt so alive.

Cole possessed her heart and soul and body . . . magnificently. He was big and masterful, leading her, stronger than she, and it was what she wanted. She had always known only a strong man could ever be important to her. It had even crossed her mind the first time she met Cole. Had that been a premonition? A lovely glimpse of the future?

Charlie smiled, a totally female smile, and Cole noticed. His body slowed. "What are you thinking?"

Her hips lifted, luring him back into the delicious rhythm her smile had interrupted. "I think I fell in love with you the first time we met, too," she confessed.

His lips came down hungrily, and the tempo resumed. Talk was forgotten, even talk of love, lost in the heat of flawless sexuality. They reached the top of the mountain together, they soared through the heavens together, and they rested . . . fulfilled, sated . . . together.

"We have a perfection few couples attain," Cole murmured, finally breaking the satisfied silence.

"I know." Charlie sighed languorously, returning his tender kiss before he moved to the bed. Snuggled into his arms, she dared to tease. "Is that why you love me?"

"Hmm, good question. Why does one person fall in love with another?"

Charlie moved her cheek against his chest, enjoying the bristles of hair tickling her skin. "Common interests?"

Cole laughed softly. "I wanted to take you to bed almost from the first. Would you call that a common interest?"

She laughed, too, then sobered. "We do have things in common, Cole."

"Yes," he agreed, pressing a kiss to her forehead. "Our work."

"The mill is very important to me."

"I know."

"Do you mind?"

Cole drew in a long breath, then admitted, "I did for a while. It's crazy how a man's mind works sometimes, Charlie. I admired your spunk and independence, even while I was doing my best to undermine it."

Startled, she sat up. "You didn't really try to undermine it, did you?"

"Not consciously." Cole's gaze washed over her, lingering at the ripe fullness of her breasts. "You're a beautiful woman, Charlie. I wanted to take care of you. Can you understand that?"

She nodded thoughtfully. "I sensed something like that. Did I rebel at that, Cole? I've always taken care of myself. Even before Dad died, I was an independent person."

"It's all right, sweetheart. I came to grips with your need for independence before today." A gentle smile curved Cole's lips. "I fell in love with an independent woman, and I wouldn't change her if I could." He brought a hand up to her face and traced a feathery line along her cheek. "I want to marry you, Charlie."

An electric current jolted her every nerve. Had her thoughts and hopes gone that far? Marriage was the logical conclusion to love in her mind, but everyone didn't feel that way. Jim had asked Cassie to live with him, and Charlie knew other couples who'd chosen that life-style over marriage. But Cole felt as she did, and it lifted her happiness to new heights. "I want to marry you, too," she replied unsteadily, fearful again of tears she really didn't want to shed at this beautiful moment.

Cole urged her down, tucked a pillow beneath her head and looked deeply into her eyes. "Soon, Charlie."

"Yes, soon," she agreed huskily.

"I want you living in this house. I want you having my babies. I want us to be together."

"Yes . . . to all those things," she whispered, nearly overcome with joy.

His mouth touched hers in a lovely, soft way, conveying love and caring. He looked at her then. "We'll share everything, Charlie. I never want another situation where you'll feel the need to keep something from me."

"Like my land trade," she murmured.

"Yes. And like Rick threatening you. I wish I'd known about that while he was still around. I guarantee he wouldn't have walked away from the mess he created quite so easily. I thought long and hard about turning him over to the law, but after talking to the loggers he fleeced I could see they were just glad Rick had been found out. He's damned lucky he didn't get a liberal dose of Montana justice from those men."

Charlie agreed with a nod. "I'm surprised he got away with it for two years. People around here don't go for his brand of con games."

"Well, he just got too smug, sweetheart. Telling you about it was a mistake he'll regret forever. I've notified every major timber operator in the country and he'll never get a supervisory job again."

"I should have told you about his threat." Charlie touched his mouth and he nibbled at her fingertips. "I love your mouth," she whispered, adoring the responsive light in his eyes that her words created.

Cole gathered her into a feverish embrace. "The thought of having you in my bed every night makes me pretty damned hot," he whispered in her ear.

She smiled, warmed with pleasure. "Hot is what I like."

"Do you think you'll like a husband who can't keep his hands off you?"

"No, I won't like him. I'll love him," she teased.

He chuckled softly and kissed her, a long, loving kiss that fogged her brain. She opened her eyes to see Cole staring down at her. "What, darling?" she asked, stroking his cheek.

"Before we get involved again in what is definitely going to be our favorite pastime, sweetheart, what about your oversized timber?"

Charlie's smile grew dimmer, but she kept her gaze steady. "I'd like to sell it, of course. George Morrison said if my land was logged and reforested properly, I would never run out of timber again. That means selective harvesting by age and size."

She paused, remembering that Cole, too, had a problem to overcome. "What will you do with your small logs now?" she asked, praying this turn of conversation wouldn't cause dissension.

"I was planning to add a small-log mill to the plant. But now . . ." Cole paused and grinned. "It'll all be in the family, won't it?"

"Why, yes, you're right," Charlie replied, getting her first real sense of what being married to Cole would entail. Just being with him was all she'd thought of, all she'd wanted, and it was almost a shock to suddenly realize she would be Mrs. Cole Morgan, a visible and distinct part of Canfield Lumber Company!

The local gossips would swoon from pure bliss over having such a delicious topic to bandy around.

Smiling at the thought, Charlie curled her fingers into the hair on the back of Cole's head. "Are you suggesting a merger, darling?" she asked seductively.

A sensual flame rekindled in his eyes. "I think we've already agreed on the merger, sweetheart. All we've got left to do is decide on some of the terms."

"And your proposal of terms?"

Cole looked a little more serious. "Stop me if you don't agree," he said. "But I can easily visualize a working partnership, with you handling all of our small timber and me dealing with the large."

He'd said *our* small timber. Already he was thinking of them as a couple, a man and woman on the same wavelength. It wasn't the timber or the promise of a more carefree professional future that thrilled Charlie; it was that one tiny word—"our."

She pulled him down to her in a burst of love. "Your terms are wonderful," she whispered raggedly. "I can visualize working together, too."

Cole's hands began to roam. "I want us to share everything, Charlie, our love, our home, our life, our businesses."

"Oh, yes, darling," she breathed happily. "Independence can only go so far."

HARLEQUIN Temptation

COMING NEXT MONTH

Have You Ever Wondered If You Could Write A Harlequin Novel?

Here's great news—Harlequin is offering a series of cassette tapes to help you do just that. Written by Harlequin editors, these tapes give practical advice on how to make your characters—and your story—come alive. There's a tape for each contemporary romance series Harlequin publishes.

Mail order only

All sales final

TO: *Harlequin Reader Service*
Audiocassette Tape Offer
P.O. Box 1396
Buffalo, NY   14269-1396

I enclose a check/money order payable to HARLEQUIN READER SERVICE® for $9.70 ($8.95 plus 75¢ postage and handling) for EACH tape ordered for the total sum of $_____*
Please send:

☐ Romance and Presents   ☐ Intrigue
☐ American Romance   ☐ Temptation
☐ Superromance   ☐ All five tapes ($38.80 total)

Signature_____
Name:_____
                                    (please print clearly)
Address:_____
State:_____ Zip:_____

* Iowa and New York residents add appropriate sales tax.

AUDIO-H

Janet DAILEY

THE MASTER FIDDLER

Jacqui didn't want to go back to college, and she didn't want to go home. Tombstone, Arizona, wasn't in her plans, either, until she found herself stuck there en route to L.A. after ramming her car into rancher Choya Barnett's Jeep. Things got worse when she lost her wallet and couldn't pay for the repairs. The mechanic wasn't interested when she practically propositioned him to get her car back—but Choya was. He took care of her bills and then waited for the debt to be paid with the only thing Jacqui had to offer—her virtue.

Watch for this bestselling Janet Dailey favorite, coming in June from Harlequin.

Also watch for *Something Extra* in August and *Sweet Promise* in October.

ANNOUNCING . . .

The Lost Moon Flower
by Bethany Campbell

Look for it this August
wherever Harlequins are sold

HR 3000-1